Tangled Webb

By the same author
The Seventeenth Swap
The Money Room
Hideaway
The Trouble with Jacob
The Striped Ships

(*Margaret K. McElderry Books*)

TANGLED WEBB

Eloise McGraw

MARGARET K. McELDERRY BOOKS
New York

Maxwell Macmillan Canada
Toronto

Maxwell Macmillan International
New York   Oxford   Singapore   Sydney

Margaret K. McElderry Books
Macmillan Publishing Company
866 Third Avenue
New York, NY 10022

Maxwell Macmillan Canada, Inc.
1200 Eglinton Avenue East
Suite 200
Don Mills, Ontario M3C 3N1

Macmillan Publishing Company is part of the Maxwell
Communication Group of Companies.

First edition   Printed in the United States of America
10 9 8 7 6 5 4 3 2 1

Library of Congress Cataloging-in-Publication Data
McGraw, Eloise Jarvis.
    Tangled Webb / by Eloise McGraw. — 1st ed.
        p.   cm.
    Summary: Twelve-year-old Juniper Webb and her best friend
Alison find themselves enmeshed in a "tangled web" when the two
girls begin to investigate Juniper's new stepmother's background.
    ISBN 0-689-50573-6
    [1. Stepmothers—Fiction.   2. Mystery and detective stories.]
I. Title.
PZ7.M47853Tan   1993
[Fic]—dc20   92-27911

To
Flo Carr, Susan Fletcher, Ellen Howard,
Marian Martin, Milena McGraw,
Winifred Morris, Dorothy Morrison,
and Marge Zimmerman
the best of critics, and the best of friends

Oh, what a tangled web we weave,
When first we practice to deceive!

—Sir Walter Scott, *Marmion*

1

There's something funny about Daddy's new wife.

Kelsey, her name is. And that's what I'm calling her, not "Mother," because Margo was my mother, and she's dead, and nobody else could be Margo, ever.

I didn't call Margo "Mother" either because she said it made her feel like somebody else, but I can *imagine* doing it. I can't even imagine calling Kelsey that. She hardly looks much older than me, though Daddy says she's twenty-five. I don't mean she *acts* like a kid, at all. But she sure looks younger than she is. Of course, I look older than twelve, Alison says—in fact, everybody says. I guess it must be true. I always hope they mean I look sort of mature and sophisticated, like high school kids. But I have a feeling it's only because I'm the tallest girl in the seventh grade. I tower over Alison, and she's already thirteen. I'm even taller than most of the boys.

Oh, well.

About Kelsey. I don't know what it is, exactly. I keep trying to put my finger on it, because it bothers me. I mean, I thought we were going to like each other. And what if we don't?

I *did* like her that first evening, when Daddy took us both out to dinner so I could meet her. She's real pretty—no, that

1

sounds too fluffy. She's real *good-looking*, in a sort of outdoorsy, natural way—though not fascinating and beautiful like Margo was—and kind of thin and dark-haired, which *is* like Margo. And her face is—I don't know—interesting. The expressions keep changing. You can practically tell what she's thinking, or at least how she's feeling, from one second to the next. It makes you want to keep watching. I could see right away why Daddy took to her. Besides, he told me she's an old-movie freak, same as he is. Charlie Chaplin, Laurel and Hardy, Buster Keaton—he loves stuff like that, and so does she; they found that out the very first day they got acquainted. I guess the same things strike them funny.

She's not as laid back as Daddy is, though. She has this kind of breathless laugh; it kind of bothered me that first evening. I kept wanting to tell her to relax, I wasn't going to bite. I know now she's just a sort of uptight person, though you can see her trying not to be. But I could tell she and Daddy both felt easy with each other—and that he really loved to be with her. Anybody could have seen from a mile off that she thought *he* was about perfect.

I was *not* jealous, either. I was *glad* Daddy had finally found somebody he wanted to go out with more than once, because like Alison's mother says, he's still a young man and shouldn't be acting middle-aged. (Actually he's already thirty-five going on thirty-six, but maybe she doesn't know that.)

Anyway, Kelsey has the kind of smile that makes you smile back whether you were planning to or not, which got us off to a good start, and she acted like she was glad to meet me, and asked a lot of questions about school, and my friends, and what I liked to do and all—not being nosy, but as if she really wanted to know, so I told her. And she told me about her little boy, two and a half years old, whose name is Preston. In fact, we got along just great.

Of course I didn't know Daddy was going to actually *marry* her and bring her and Preston right into our house to live with us. Maybe I wouldn't have been so enthusiastic if I'd realized that—and how soon it was all going to happen. I mean, he'd only known her for a month or so. But he says it wasn't even a week before he was wanting to take care of her forever.

Well, and maybe I'd have been all for it, anyway. Especially after I'd seen Preston.

But now there's this other thing. I can't tell exactly what it is. It's just the way Kelsey acts sometimes. Like she just all at once closes a door in your face, right while she's smiling.

Maybe she's just nervous about me, or something. Daddy said she might be. Scared I wouldn't like her—because of Margo. Well, I'm all *ready* to like her, if she'll let me. But she'd better begin letting me! She's had nearly three weeks now since the wedding. The first week, of course, they were down at the beach on their honeymoon, while I stayed over at Alison's. Some honeymoon, Alison said—with a two-year-old along! Well, I *did* offer to keep him. I wouldn't have minded. I've baby-sat with little tiny kids lots of times. Daddy could even have got old Mrs. Evans, who used to baby-sit me, to come stay with both of us. But Kelsey acted kind of panicky at the very idea. It's like she can't bear to be separated from Preston.

I guess I shouldn't blame her for that, though I've noticed most parents grab the chance to get away from their two-year-olds for a little while. She's just different, I guess. I'll probably understand when we get better acquainted.

If we ever do.

That's what's bothering me, really. I can't see we're making any progress—and it's not my fault. Maybe she wants to know *me*, the way she's always saying. She seems to mean it. But I don't think she wants me to know *her*.

And I don't know how I feel about that.

Evening

I was writing all that in this new Blankbook during English class today—well, I'd finished my essay, and I've been dying to start on this book because I just love the red leather binding. Vinyl, I mean. I think it's the prettiest one of all the Blankbooks I've had. It's recycled paper too.

Anyway, I'd sort of forgotten where I was, and all at once I heard, "JUNIPER WEBB!" in Ms. Davis's worst voice.

Of course my insides jumped, and my hands did a sort of magician's trick all by themselves, stuffing the Blankbook into my ring binder out of sight; and all the time I was saying real innocently, "Yes, Ms. Davis?"

"Essays! I'm calling for the essays!"

I mumbled, "Oh—sure—sorry," and snatched up my two pages and headed for her desk, bucking the traffic, since everybody else in the class was on the way back to their seats.

"Stay with us, Juniper," Ms. Davis said in this perfectly mild, amiable tone, and tossed my essay onto the stack. "I don't blame you for wanting to fill these odd quarter-hours you spend waiting for everybody else, but—you *are* in class. Keep in touch," she added.

I mumbled something else and went back to my seat as inconspicuously as I could, which wasn't very, of course. Alison rolled her eyes, questioning me, as I passed her. The whites just glistened against that bitter-chocolate skin of hers. I wish I had dark eyes, and at least sort of *olive* skin, like

4

Margo's. No luck, I'm just like Daddy, only without the beard—speckled-green eyes and hair-colored hair. Oh, well.

I wiggled my eyebrows at Alison and shrugged, since I wasn't sure whether I'd got a telling off or a bucking up. Telling off for inattention, maybe. Bucking up for smarts. Smarts in English, anyway. I have *no problem* with idle quarter-hours in math.

The bell rang about then, and we all slapped our books together and surged out into the hall, which was deafening as usual. The minute we got to our lockers Alison yelled, "So what did she say?" real apprehensively. Ms. Davis always fills Alison with apprehension.

I told her, "Nothing much," but she shivered dramatically as she yanked her locker door open. "It's the *way* she says it."

"Yes, but she wasn't being sarcastic this time. I *was* goofing off."

"Doing what?"

I actually had my mouth open to answer, then closed it and got busy stowing my books away. I don't know why, but all at once I knew I wasn't going to show Alison this new Blankbook. The old ones were different; they're just full of silly verses and long descriptions of sunsets and copied-out jokes and drawings and who likes who and stuff. I mean, we've both been filling Blankbooks ever since we gave each other one for Christmas when we were nine years old, and sharing them same as we've shared almost everything else since third grade. But this one suddenly felt private. I mumbled, "Just doodling," and told her to grab her jacket or we'd miss the bus.

We both got off at my stop, though Alison's apartment—well, her mother's—is three blocks farther on. We nearly always go to my house whenever Alison doesn't have her clarinet lesson or ballet practice or drama club or an orthodontist's appointment or some other dumb thing. There's nobody home either place till five o'clock or so—her mom works at a real estate office clear downtown—but she hates to go into an empty apartment. I can't understand why. I just love to walk up Daddy's curving flagstone path that he made himself, to our red front door—it was Margo who painted it red—and get out my own house key, and give it that special little wiggle-twist you have to do to make the lock work, and then lead the way in, and sniff the sort of faint ghost-of-breakfast smell that comes out to meet me. It makes me feel more grown-up, the person half in charge of the house—equal partners with Daddy.

Of course, I'm not, anymore. Everything's different. Which I had been almost about to forget this afternoon.

I stopped halfway down the slope of our street to the dead end where our house is, hugging my books and wondering if I should warn Alison. She hasn't been over since the wedding. Last week we both had hockey practice and that journalism club meeting. And the week before had still been the honeymoon.

"Kelsey'll be there today, you know," I said. "Preston may not have waked up from his nap and she'll want us to be quiet."

Alison said, kind of surprised, "Well, that's okay, we're not going to yell and scream, are we? I'd just as soon begin on that math together. Then when he wakes up can we play with him?"

"If Kelsey doesn't mind."

"Mind? My cousin Tracy *pays* me to come play with Sammy, just to keep him out from under her feet." Alison giggled as we started on. "I can't wait to see him! Preston, I mean."

"You did see him!"

"Only for about two seconds."

I guess it was just a glimpse—at the little reception down in the church rec room after the wedding. And she barely met Kelsey. There wasn't time for much socializing before Daddy said they had to start for the coast. Actually it was a kind of dim reception, just church punch and a sheet cake, with mostly Daddy's friends and some of his longtime computer customers, and two women from where Kelsey worked. She's only lived in Oregon since last fall and hardly knows anybody.

"How d'you like her by now?" Alison asked me. "I mean— is she nice?"

"Sure she's nice!" I said. "D'you think Daddy'd marry somebody who wasn't nice?"

"Well, I mean—*you* know. Do you *like* her?"

I said, "Sure! Of course."

Maybe I shouldn't've said it so fast, or so loud, or something, because Alison gave me the kind of look that tells me she's suddenly thinking questions. I just pretended I didn't notice. Anyway, I *do* like Kelsey. I added, real casually, "I don't know her very well yet."

"Well, naturally not! How could you? After all, it's only been about—not even a month." Alison shifted her books to her other arm and added, "I hope you've got something edible in your refrigerator. I'm starving."

I'm no good at pretending. She knows there's something wrong. Maybe she even knows I'm not exactly sure yet what it is. But Alison's not like some people. She won't bug me to talk about it until I'm ready.

I stopped at the box to get the mail, dumped it on top of my ring binder and books, and sorted it one-handed as we walked up the flagstone path. Junk, two envelopes with windows, and three letters from Gramma—one to Daddy, one to Kelsey, and one to me.

I said, "Goody!" and reached for the doorknob, but before I could turn it, the door opened and Kelsey stepped out so suddenly we nearly crashed into each other.

"*Oh!*" she gasped. "Oh—hi, Juniper! I'm sorry! You startled me." She backed up, almost stumbling, and swung the door wide, smiling but looking all flustered. She was wearing a coral T-shirt, and she'd gone so pink her cheeks nearly matched it. She looked startled, all right, a lot more so than I could see much reason for. She went on talking, kind of fast. "I was just going out to see if the mail had—oh, good, you've got it. Not that I'm expecting anything . . ." She took the envelopes I handed her, looking uncertainly at Alison. "Hi . . . Alice?"

Alison just grinned and said, "Alison Fisher."

"*Alison.* Sorry! I'm awful at remembering names. I do know who you are, honest. Juniper's best friend. Come on in."

"You've got a letter from Gramma," I told her. "We each got one."

"Oh!" Kelsey closed the door, studying the envelopes in her hand. "From Bozeman, Montana. That's your father's mother, isn't it? She's writing *me?*"

"Probably saying, 'Welcome to the family,' or something."

"How nice!" Kelsey's color had begun to fade enough so you could see the freckles across her nose and cheekbones, but now she flushed up again. It wasn't because she was pleased, though. She was looking at that envelope as if it might bite her.

She couldn't be nervous about *Gramma?* She wouldn't be if she knew her. I said, "You'll like Gramma," sort of to reassure her. "She's a lot like Daddy. Kind of quiet and easygoing. But doesn't *give* when you push. You know."

"Yes, I know," Kelsey said, and she gave me a look I couldn't figure out at all. She smiled a little, as if she were going to say something else, but she didn't. She just tucked the letter in her pocket and said, "Come on in the kitchen. I made cookies this morning. Only keep it down, Preston's still asleep."

It still seems funny to see her moving around our kitchen, twitching aside Margo's curtains with the red roosters on them, and using Margo's favorite coffee mug and my cookie plate with the scalloped edge that I bought that time at the beach with my allowance, that Margo always saved for when *I* made brownies. I kept having to swallow little objections or, anyway, comments that I'd probably have been sorry about later. The trouble is, the whole kitchen still seems like Margo's, even after all these years. Probably because Daddy and I never changed anything. Maybe Kelsey will, now. Maybe she should.

The cookies were the ones on the back of the oatmeal box— I guess Kelsey doesn't know many recipes. But she put in chocolate chips instead of raisins, and it made them real good. By the time I'd read my letter—and then read it again because it sounded just like Gramma and was almost like talking to her—Alison was halfway through her milk and gabbing away to Kelsey as if they were old pals. Alison's old pals with everybody in five minutes if you give her half a chance. There I was just reaching for my second cookie and she was already telling Kelsey all about Author Day next Tuesday, and Elizabeth Kenilworth coming to give talks, and that she—I mean Alison—is going to write books, too, when she grows up, and she's going to ask Elizabeth Kenilworth all about how to do it when she goes up afterward to get her autograph.

As if anybody could just tell you, in about two sentences, how to write books. Alison's sure to ask, though. And whatever Elizabeth Kenilworth answers, she'll put it all down in her notebook. Alison is really absolutely sure she's going to be a great author when she's about Kelsey's age. Well, maybe I'd like that too, I mean I *know* I would. But I have trouble believing I'll ever write all that well. To tell the truth, I have trouble believing Alison will. I mean, her plots are so sort of *wild.*

Anyway, Kelsey asked what kind of books Elizabeth Kenilworth writes, and that's when one of those odd things happened again. Alison said, "Mysteries!" and gave one of her movie-actor shivers and started listing titles. I think she owns about ten of the books. "*The Tale of the Tower. Three Blind Bats. The Secret of the Old Well.* Oooo, they're wonderful!"

Kelsey smiled and said, "Scary?"

"Well—*fun* scary. I mean—"

Alison bogged down, so I helped. "Not scary like vampires and monsters. Scary because something bad's bound to happen and you don't know when. Or somebody's out to get you but you don't know who."

Alison gave one of her bubbly giggles. "Yeah. It's like a sledgehammer hung up somewhere waiting to fall on your head."

There was a little tiny pause, then Kelsey said, "That's fun?" in an odd sort of voice that made me stare.

Alison blinked, and said, "Well—you know. It's only a book."

By then Kelsey was laughing in that breathless way she has. She said, "Oh, sure, I know. It really sounds like a good read." She was still smiling as she got up to refill the cookie plate, which didn't need refilling. But she'd closed that door behind the smile.

I don't think Alison noticed. She just went on about Elizabeth Kenilworth, while I watched Kelsey and wondered what there could have been in that silly conversation to bother anybody. Then in a minute here came little splatting footsteps along the bare floor of the hall, and Preston showed up in the kitchen doorway. He just stood there in his undershirt grinning at us, and he's so *cute*, with his curly little dark mop and brown eyes, and *one* dimple, that we all forgot whatever we'd been thinking about, and just concentrated on him. He's going to be one spoiled little kid if we don't watch out—with me and Kelsey and Daddy and now Alison, too, all crazy about him. He sure does look like Kelsey—no doubt about whose little boy he is. He's even got a few little brown freckles like hers, right across his button of a nose.

She didn't mind at all if Alison and I played with him, so we got him dressed and took him out in his stroller for a while, only not far, not even down to the mall. Kelsey doesn't let him much out of her sight. He learned to say "Alsnfisher," and he kept sort of patting Alison's hand or arm, in a surprised sort of way. I guess he hasn't known many black people. Then we brought him home again and helped him build block towers till Alison had to leave. We never did do any math.

Kelsey is okay, really, I've decided. Some people are just not as cool as others, that's all. Kelsey's one of the jumpy ones. Meeting strangers, like Daddy's friends or even Alison, and sudden surprises like when we nearly collided in the doorway—things like that throw her off balance for a minute. Once she gets used to living here—in Margo's house—and being married again, she's bound to get over it and act like anybody else. Probably she thinks everybody's criticizing her and comparing her to Margo. They probably are too. I guess I am. I ought to try to quit.

Oh, well. It's only about three weeks since the wedding. It'll all wear off. It's bound to. Things are going to be perfectly okay.

2

I don't know. Things are *not* perfectly okay. I wish I could tell whether it's my fault or Kelsey's. I can't decide whether to feel guilty or not.

Daddy sticks up for Kelsey, of course. I mean, he sort of keeps explaining her to me. I listen too. I *want* her explained. But the things he explains never seem exactly the same things I'm bothered about.

Oh, well, quit *talking* about it.

Daddy's gone until tomorrow evening. He had to go down to Klamath Falls to do something for that big office down there where he installed all their computers a couple of years ago. They're always having problems and yelling for help. If they'd only bought better systems they wouldn't have so much trouble, and neither would he, but they insisted on these elcheapo printers and software so what can you expect? I tell Daddy he ought to take a couple of weekdays off to make up for working weekends, but he'll never do that. And if you're a one-man business you can't send anybody in your place.

I used to like it when he had to drive to some other town on the weekend, because he always took me with him—after Margo died, I mean. If he had to go on school days, of course

13

Mrs. Evans came and stayed with me, but Saturdays I always went along, and we had the best time, singing dumb songs and counting mailboxes and playing animal-vegetable-mineral and stuff like that. And I always talked to him. It was a chance to tell him about whatever was on my mind. Then, while he was working on the systems, I sat in whatever office it was and did my homework, and we had dinner at a restaurant and slept at a motel. It was really fun.

Now there's no need for me to go along because Kelsey's always here to be with me and fix meals and stuff. She's home all the time—she quit her job when they got married. Instead, she's taken over the job Daddy's answering service used to do.

It was so she wouldn't have to leave Preston at Tiny Tots Day-Care Center anymore, and I don't blame her, really. He's so *little* to leave with people he doesn't know. Kelsey said he never would say a word to anybody at Tiny Tots, for the whole time he stayed there—nearly five months. She thinks it made him slower to begin talking. He doesn't say much, even now, to anybody but her. I've heard him chattering away to her—not that he has much of a vocabulary yet—but if Daddy or I or Alison or anybody else comes into the room, he shuts right up. He'll smile, and play blocks or pat-a-cake with you, and say your name if you ask "Who am I?" He's quick and smart as anything. But he just won't talk much. He calls me "Juper."

Kelsey told me she likes my name. It was last night at dinner, and I was trying to get Preston to say "Ju-ni-per," only he wouldn't, just grinned at me with his mouth full of mashed potatoes as if I was making a real funny joke. And Kelsey all of a sudden said, "I just love your name. It's so *unusual*. Was it your idea, Charley, or—" She stopped, as if she maybe wished she hadn't asked Daddy that.

But he just said, "No, it was Margo's. One weekend not long before Juni was born, she and I drove over into central Oregon, down along the Deschutes—"

I got up quick and took my plate to the kitchen so I wouldn't have to listen. Margo must've told me that story a hundred times when I was little—about the smell of juniper that was everywhere, even in the towns, and her deciding right then that she wanted a spicy, sharp, lively little girl just like that spicy, sharp, lively fragrance—and that she'd got one. I used to make her tell me that over and over, whenever I thought about it. It made me feel so special.

But I could hardly stand Daddy sharing that sort of real private thing about Margo with *Kelsey*. I feel like it ought to stay just something between him and me, a part of remembering Margo. I don't know. Maybe I'm wrong to feel that way.

Anyway, last night when Kelsey was putting Preston to bed, I grabbed my chance and went into the little office room where Daddy'd been returning his customers' phone calls, and asked him straight out if he was going to talk about Margo to Kelsey. I mean, I was nice about it, but there wasn't time to lead up to it gradually, or be tactful.

He swiveled his chair around right away, looking startled and real concerned. But he misunderstood me totally. "Juni, you mustn't worry about anything like that!" he said. "Kelsey would *never* get jealous. She's the most generous person in the world. It was something I noticed about her right off." Before I could say a word, he went right on, reaching out to move his visitor's chair so I could sit up close to him. He can handle a heavy wooden chair with one big hand, easy, as if it didn't weigh anything. "Jealousy just isn't in her nature. She knows very well Margo was irreplaceable—for you and me both. We've talked about it—she understands perfectly, and doesn't want it any other way."

I said, "Well, but I didn't mean—I mean—" I don't know what I was trying to say. We were just suddenly on a different subject and I couldn't think how to get us back.

Daddy said, "It's a little hard to explain it to you. My years with Margo just seem a separate part of my life now. Another world." He stared at nothing for a minute, maybe back into that other world, because he got this expression on his face that it used to have when he looked at Margo—a kind of amused but marveling look, as if he were watching a magic show. Then he blinked that away and focused on me again, rubbing his knuckles back and forth under his beard. It's short and wiry and sandy colored, blonder than his hair. The light from the desk lamp made a kind of halo around its edges. He said, "All I can say is Kelsey and I have a different feeling for each other from the one I had for Margo, or Kelsey had for Tim. It's a second marriage for her, too, remember. It's calmer. But very secure. I'm gonna make sure of that."

"Yes, sure," I mumbled. "I realize. But I—"

"She needs badly to feel secure. She's got a lot of courage, but she's had a rough time, you know, on her own, with a tiny baby, and all."

"I know." He'd told me before about Kelsey's first husband—Tim Blockman his name was. She married this Tim Blockman right out of high school, but after Preston was born the marriage kind of fell apart, and Tim Blockman went off and joined the Coast Guard, and was drowned in a rescue mission during a storm. I guess it was a bad time, all right. I said, "I want to be friends, Daddy. Honest. But it seems like she sort of—pulls back or something."

"Give her time, Juni. She hasn't much self-confidence yet

and—she's unduly nervous. Especially about you, I think. That's all it is."

Explaining Kelsey to me again. I wonder if he ever tries to explain me to Kelsey. I hope not. I mean, if Kelsey can't trust me and be friends without a lot of explanations and coaching, then forget it. I don't want her to *pretend*. In fact there are things I don't specially want explained.

I gave up trying to talk about it. I could hear Kelsey upstairs fetching Preston's final drink of water, so the conversation was over anyway.

When she came down I helped her load the dishwasher and even watched TV with her for a while so I wouldn't feel guilty about anything. But after Daddy finished his calls and joined us, I said something about homework and sloped on upstairs to my room, and flopped onto my old beanbag chair and sat there remembering things about Margo—I mean on purpose, even when it hurt to remember, even though I knew very well I'd feel worse afterward, not better. It was like shutting myself in a closet to eat a whole box of chocolates.

For instance I went over all the made-up stories she used to tell me, at bedtime or when she was doing something boring like making jam and wanted to entertain us both while she worked. I was just a little kid then, of course—she died when I was barely eight—so they were little-kid stories. One was about a bug named James and another one about a goldfish named Swoosh, and she could just *be* a bug or a goldfish—or a bear or a king, or anything. She never just *told* stories, or just read them, either. She acted them out. Well, she was an actress—semiprofessional, she used to call it, because she didn't work all the time; but she was a member of Actors Equity, and could land a part just about any time she tried,

17

here with the Hillridge Players or with any other of the little theaters in the Portland area. She usually did one play in the summer and one in winter, with about a month's run each. And Daddy always took me to see any play she was in, even if it was something I was a lot too young for, like *Hedda Gabler* or *The Seagull*; all I remember about that one was asking Daddy in a loud voice if somebody wasn't going to bury that big dead bird and people in the seats around us snickering.

She used to teach me little dance routines too, and the songs to go with them, and we'd do them together in the living room or out in our backyard. I bet I could still do a couple of them, but it wouldn't be the same without Margo mugging away beside me. I know I could still cue anybody for the second scene, third act of *A Midsummer Night's Dream*, which I loved so much Daddy took me to see it three times. Margo played Puck, and she was just *magical*, she really was. And once she played the heroine of a real crazy melodrama called *They Shan't Take the Farm*, and we could all recite bits of that. Daddy and I still go through this dumb little ritual—a kind of family joke—that started when she was learning her lines. Whenever anybody happens to ask, "Where are you going?"—which people ask oftener than you'd think—one of us automatically says, "Out of your life, forever!" Then the other says, "I'd kill to stop you!" And the other shrieks, "You mean—?" And the last line is "I mean your lover, Richard!" That's the sequence, and we can't seem to stop till we get to the end, even if we're in a hurry, or not in a silly mood, or in some public place like an elevator and have to gabble through it under our breath. Margo could do it in a piercing whisper.

I guess people must've thought we were mental, sometimes, the three of us. But it was so much fun.

Oh, well. It's over. I wish I'd quit thinking about it. I don't, usually. I mean, it's not like me to *brood*. I guess it's because of all that last night about my name, and trying to talk to Daddy later and making a flub of it.

I still want to tell him what I really meant. But it's hard to get him alone. Maybe he and I could go for a walk some evening the way we used to, and I could bring it up again, and do it better. I mean, I don't want to be a snerp, or create a big problem or anything. And I don't want to *exclude* Kelsey. Exactly. But I just feel some things ought to stay mine, and Daddy's, and Margo's. And nobody else's.

I hear Kelsey and Preston coming in from the backyard. She's been planting petunias this morning. Preston's probably been making mud pies. *I'm* supposed to be cleaning my room, and I better get at it.

SUNDAY, MAY 19

Alison came over after lunch today so we could do math together, and between us we managed to work all but three problems of that extra-big review assignment. And guess what—Kelsey helped us with the last three! She happened to walk through the dining room when we were slaving away and asking each other how to get square roots and divide fractions, and a lot of other obviously lamebrain questions, and she stopped and answered some of them, then sat down and looked at the stuff we were stuck on, and straightened us right out. I guess she and Daddy do have a lot in common— more than just old movies. They have sort of the same kind of minds. I mean, math is actually *fun* to them.

I said, "Thank you," and so did Alison, and we really meant it. I did, anyway, because I think I'll always remember about square roots now. Alison doesn't *want* to remember them a minute after school's out. I asked, "But what if you need to know about them sometime?" and she said she intends to plan her life so she *won't* need to. She'll get an A in math, though. She works hardest at stuff she's bad at. *I* think you ought to work hardest at stuff you're good at, so you can get even better. We argue about it all the time.

Anyway, after we'd finished we all three kept on sitting there at the table—Preston was down for his nap—and Alison said she was going to spend the last three weeks of August with her father in Minneapolis. Her dad and mom have been divorced a long time, but Alison visits him once a year. He works in a men's store there, and plays clarinet in the Minneapolis Symphony, and they have outdoor summer concerts, and she gets to go to them.

"I'm glad Mom and I don't live there anymore, though," she said. "It's so *cold* in winter. Pop grew up in Minnesota, so he's used to it."

"I grew up right in this house," I said. "Where did you, Kelsey?" I mean, because of the math I was feeling all friendly and like I knew Kelsey a little better, and didn't even ask myself if that was the sort of question that might make her act funny.

It was, though. She gave me this startled look and then looked down at her hands, and picked up my math book and put it exactly straight on top of my ring binder, and said real fast, "Oh, up north."

Alison asked, "You mean Washington? Hey, that's where my mother grew up!" She sounded as if that made them long-lost relatives or something. "Mom went clear through high school in Bellingham, Washington. That's about as far north as you can get and still be in the U.S.A.!" she added, laughing about it, not meaning anything at all.

Kelsey stiffened up and said, "No, it wasn't Bellingham! It was east of there—a good ways. Just a little place; you probably never heard of it." Then she said, "Oh! I forgot! I was going to wash that lettuce," and was out of there and running water in the kitchen before we could say another word.

Alison and I sort of looked at each other, and then she gathered up her books and said she'd better get on home, and did I want to walk as far as the 7-Eleven with her and get a Coke. Well, I said okay, but I wasn't much in the mood, to tell you the truth. I mean, after being all helpful and everything, Kelsey'd just slammed that door again, for no reason.

We'd hardly got to the end of the walk before Alison asked, "Was it me saying 'Bellingham,' or what? What was the matter?"

"I don't know. Something is." I've gone about as long as I can without talking to Alison about it.

"How come she didn't want to tell us the name of that little place, I wonder? D'you s'pose it's real grungy or something?"

"Maybe there isn't any such place," I said.

"You mean she was just making it *up*?"

"Sounded like it. Sounded like she couldn't think of a good name for a town. Maybe she grew up someplace else entirely, and just didn't want to tell us."

"But that's so—that's so—" Alison groped for a word and came out with "peculiar." I didn't say anything, and after a while she asked in an interested voice, "*Why* would anybody want to lie about where she grew up and went to school?"

I said, "Are you really asking me, or are you going to tell me?" Alison loves to make up theories about people. She calls it Analyzing Character.

"I'm going to tell you some possibilities. Then you tell me

21

some. Okay. People lie because they don't want to tell the truth. *Why* don't they want to tell the truth? Ashamed to, maybe."

"Scared to," I contributed.

"Yeah! That's better! Only, scared of what? Lemme see. Maybe she's got a police record."

"In a little tiny town east of Bellingham, Washington?"

"Well, it might be big enough to have a police officer. And anyhow, she might *really* be from Seattle, or L.A., or anywhere. New York! Maybe some Mafia gang is after her!"

"Oh, that's bound to be it. She's the Godfather's grand-daughter and he wanted to teach Preston to peddle crack, so she ran away."

"Or—I'll tell you. This is *it*, really. She's from outer space. She *can't* tell us, see? We wouldn't even believe her."

"You're right! That's why she's so good at math, doing all that spaceship navigation, but she doesn't dare let anybody know because. . . ." I forget how I finished that one.

By this time we were almost to the 7-Eleven and were breaking each other up. I guess it wasn't really all that scream-ingly witty, now I write it down. But at least we managed to sweep the whole subject under the rug. For a while, anyway.

3

Today was Author Day, and it was *lots* more interesting than I thought it was going to be. Last year when Thomas Terry came it wasn't all that great. He sort of yammered on and on, and never really said anything you could remember afterward.

But Elizabeth Kenilworth is *good*. I've only read one or two of her books, but I'm going to read them *all* now. In fact I went to the library during lunch break and checked out *The Third Owl*. She's pretty old—maybe as old as Gramma—but real lively, with sort of wispy gray-and-black hair pulled up into a knot on top of her head, and long silver earrings, and bright eyes like a squirrel. And she didn't just talk about herself and why she wrote this book or won a prize for that one, she talked about *storytelling*. Alison was right—she actually did tell us how to write books, though it took a lot more than two sentences. And Alison scribbled it all down, just like I said she would.

I have to admit I took some notes, too; Elizabeth Kenilworth made it all sound so simple. But I have a feeling that even if I did every single thing she said, I wouldn't come up with much of a best-seller. There's bound to be more to it than

23

rules and tricks and stuff—more underneath. You've got to have talent. Well, she said that. She didn't try to fool us.

I wonder if I have any talent. For anything. I never thought so, because I didn't get Margo's singing voice, or her looks—and I sure didn't get Daddy's mathematical brain. I used to dance and playact with Margo all the time, and I *felt* like I was acting, but I guess it never looked like much. Whenever they put on plays at school I usually wind up on the stage crew. The only thing I'm especially good at is English. And I wouldn't have thought writing essays on My Summer Vacation or The Louisiana Purchase was a bit like writing a book.

But one thing Elizabeth Kenilworth said today gave me kind of a different slant on the sort of books *she* writes—not essays but stories. Fiction. She said writing a story is like acting in a play *inside your head*. You take all the parts. And at the same time you're the director—watching what the actors do, and listening to them, and changing the dialogue or the action around when it isn't quite right. She said the primitive story-tellers, who were probably already around in caveman days, were the world's first dramatists.

I wonder if I could do that? Act out a play inside my head?

WEDNESDAY, MAY 22

Alison wants to start plotting a mystery book right away. She wants us *both* to do it—I mean, together. I might have known. She had to go straight from school to her orthodontist appointment yesterday so we barely got to discuss it until after dinner, but then we talked on the phone about an hour.

We were arguing, mostly. I said if we didn't even know

how to make up plots all by ourselves, how could we do it together?

She said, "It'll be *easier*! We can give each other ideas! The way we were doing the other day about Kelsey."

"Oh, hey, great. You mean 'The Mystery of the Godfather's Granddaughter'? That would be a winner."

"Well, we could think up something better about the Mafia. Something real mean and scary."

"We don't *know* anything about the Mafia."

"That doesn't matter! We can make it up. Or else—what about illegal aliens? There's this beautiful, exotic-looking girl, and she just transferred into this other girl's high school, and nobody exactly knows where she came from—"

"Not even the principal?"

"Well—she *says* she's from another town. But—"

"Doesn't she have her transcript?"

"Oh, don't be so—so—realistic! Okay, she *forged* one. And she pretends she can't speak Spanish. But one day this other girl hears her jabbering away in fluent Spanish—"

"Who to?"

"Oh, to—um—her mother. On the *phone*. And that gives her away, see? Help me think of a Spanishy name for her— Annamaria, maybe?"

"Wouldn't she forge a name, too?"

"Oh, yeah! Sure! Something *not* Spanishy."

"Molly O'Brien."

"That's too Irish! Something real *American*."

"Betsy Ross?"

"*Juniper*, come on! Don't be like that—" Alison was giggling, though, and I was too; and about then Daddy came in and told me he hated to interrupt what sounded like a serious intellectual discussion, but he had to return his customers' calls.

Later

Guess what! Kelsey now has a complete, made-up story about where she grew up. I *know* it's made up. If it's true, why didn't she tell Alison and me any of this stuff the other day?

She brought it up herself. Earlier this evening, after Daddy took over the phone, I went into the living room and turned on "The Real West Show," which I kind of like when I'm in the mood, and pretty soon she came down from putting Preston to bed and started watching too. It was a thing about Chief Joseph and the Nez Perce, and filmed in some high, deserty-looking country. Well, when it was over, Kelsey said, "Reminds me of where I grew up. Near Grand Coulee."

"Grand Coulee?" I repeated, scurrying madly around in my mind for some kind of map that would remind me where Grand Coulee is. I'm sure it's in eastern Washington, but I wouldn't have put it "up *north*," which was what she said the other day. Of course, it's north of *here*. I asked, "Isn't there a big dam at Grand Coulee?"

"A town too. We weren't right *in* the town, though. We lived in a trailer park out near the dam. My dad was a mechanic with the Army Corps of Engineers. Al-Albert Morgan." Kelsey swallowed. I could hear her do it. She was looking past me, sort of at nothing, and talking in this real casual voice as if it wasn't a bit important. Maybe it isn't. Or *wouldn't* be if she'd told us all this in the first place.

Anyhow, she went right on. They'd moved their trailer from Grand Coulee to Chief Joseph Dam, which I guess is on the

Columbia too, and then her dad worked for a while at the John Day Dam in eastern Oregon; and I guess she'd gone to high school in a couple of those places. Her mom had run off with somebody a long time before that. She doesn't know where her mom is. And then her dad was injured on the dam somehow, and died, so he was gone, too, and her brother moved to Australia, so she married this Tim Blockman. And after *he* drowned in the Coast Guard rescue, she brought Preston to the Portland area to find a better job, and ended up here in Hillridge.

I said, "I didn't even know you had a brother."

"Yeah, Bob. He's a lot older than me. I hardly knew him, really."

"How come he moved to *Australia?*"

"To raise sheep. He used to work on a sheep ranch in Idaho, summers, and he liked it."

I wondered why he couldn't raise sheep in Idaho—it seemed lots more convenient—but I didn't say so. It would've been mean to pin her down. Personally, I think she should have skipped the brother. He was just one more she had to kill off or send someplace far away so nobody could trace him. I don't believe a word of her story. I wonder if Daddy does, or if she's even filled him in on all that.

Just wait till I tell Alison!

FRIDAY, MAY 24

We had a test in social studies today. About the Egyptians. I think I only missed one question—couldn't remember which Rameses it was that built the temple at Abu Simbel. I'm sorry we're nearly through with the Egyptians; I liked them. I like that funny way they drew people—sideways from the neck up and the waist down, but with the shoulders and chest facing front. It looks great, for some weird reason. But you can't *do* it, yourself, no matter how you twist.

I didn't tell Alison about Kelsey and the Grand Coulee, after all. I don't really feel like talking about it. I mean, why can't Kelsey *trust* me? So what if she once did something she shouldn't, or somebody's after her, or whatever it is. *I* wouldn't care—and I wouldn't tell anybody, either. Maybe I'd try to *help*. I just don't like people to lie to me.

SUNDAY, MAY 26

Daddy's going to take all of us over to the Cocked Hat for a hamburger this evening, to save Kelsey cooking. She does make hard going of it, but she's trying, I'll say that for her. Yesterday I went into the kitchen for a diet Coke and there she was at the breakfast table, going through all Margo's old cookbooks. I felt sorry for her all of a sudden—she looked so sort of outnumbered. I would've said something, only I couldn't think what.

I got my Coke out of the fridge, and when I turned around she'd closed the book she'd been looking at—it was one of the big fat ones, Julia Child I think—and was smiling in this embarrassed, apologetic way.

"I thought I might study up a little," she said. "But I'm afraid the course is beyond me. I haven't had the prerequisites."

"There's lots easier recipes than the ones in there," I told her. I came over to the table and picked out a couple of the most splattered and worn-out books. "Daddy and I have been eating out of these for years. And if *he* can cook something, believe me, it's easy."

Kelsey took them, and smiled at me, and turned a few pages, but then she looked straight at me and said, "I want to learn the hard ones. *She* was a very good cook, wasn't she? Your mother. Margo."

She acted like it was hard for her to say Margo's name, as if it took *courage*. But she said it, and kept her eyes looking right into mine—not challenging or anything, just wanting me to tell her honestly.

I said, "Yes, I guess so." Actually I don't exactly know whether Margo was such a great cook. I do remember we used to have some real fancy thing with a foreign name one night, and maybe soup out of a can the next. But I was still at the age then when anything I'd never tried before was poison, so I don't think I got much benefit out of Julia Child. "I guess she was a good cook when she felt like it," I told Kelsey. "And opened a can when she didn't."

She laughed and said, "Fair enough. So long as you *have* a choice. So far all I can do is open cans. But I'll improve, don't give up."

I told her I wasn't worrying about it and I didn't think Daddy was, either, but she just said Daddy was the most patient man in the world and maybe the best one, and deserved something good to eat; and she pulled another big fat cookbook toward her. I guess she's going to pass that course or bust.

She is fond of Daddy, I know that. More than fond. She really loves him. You can see by the way she looks at him sometimes, as if she's trying to think up things good enough to do for him. I wish she'd talk to me oftener the way she did about the cookbooks—just frank and ordinary, without—well—hiding anything.

Why do I always feel she's hiding something? Maybe a lot of things. More than just where she grew up. I don't know. But she *is*.

MONDAY, MAY 27

We ran into the Bradleys over at the Cocked Hat last night—Cindy and Tom Bradley, who run the Hillridge Players Theater. I hadn't seen them in ages, and I guess Daddy hadn't, either. Well, they were mainly Margo's friends, being part of the theater bunch and all. After Margo died, naturally Daddy never went to any of those cast parties or saw people at rehearsals or anything, so we sort of lost touch with most of them, even Cindy and Tom. They were always top favorites of mine. They haven't any kids, so they used to make a big fuss over me, and bring me bits of discarded costumes to dress up in. Until just a couple of years ago I still had a cavalier's hat they gave me, with a big moth-eaten purple plume. I don't know what happened to it.

Well, anyway, we'd just started on our hamburgers when in they walked, and there was this big reunion—only it would have been a lot less complicated if we hadn't been in a crowded restaurant, standing up to say hello with our napkins in our hands and our chairs bumping the backs of our knees, and if Daddy hadn't had to introduce Kelsey right away, and explain to her who Cindy and Tom were, and to them who *she* was. Then of course they spotted Preston in the high chair—and, well, who's going to pay attention to anybody else when

30

Preston's around? He just calmly went on stuffing himself with hamburger while they fussed over him, as if he hardly knew they were there, but then he threw one of his little sideways glances up at them, and grinned so his dimple showed, so you knew he was just kidding. Flirting, that's what he does. I didn't blame them for getting hooked right away.

Only I kept waiting for them to get around to me, and they never really did. Right at first, when they were shaking hands with Daddy and saying what a long time it had been and everything, Cindy spotted me standing on the other side of the table, and said, "Is that little *Juniper?* Good heavens, honey, I can't believe how you've shot up!" which made me wish I'd stayed sitting down. But then Daddy sort of turned her around to meet Kelsey, and Tom smiled at me and asked, "How's school?" and before I could answer *he* had to turn and meet Kelsey, and in about five minutes they had to leave because they were in the way of the busboys, and people coming and going and all. So that was it.

Oh, well. I don't know what I expected. But I mean, they spent twice as much time gooing over Preston as they did talking to me, and we're *old friends*, I always thought. They used to pay more attention to me than to my folks, almost. When I was little and cute. Like Preston is now. I guess it's the "little and cute" they like, and not the person.

Yuck. Does that ever sound disgusting! As if I was *jealous* of Preston. Well, I'm not! It was just that this one time— because it was Cindy and Tom. That's no excuse, is it? So, okay, maybe for a minute, just tonight, my nose was out of joint—that's what Gramma would say.

If I'm going to be that kind of a snerp I'll just have to get over it. Nobody twelve years old and practically seven feet tall—well, five-six-and-a-half, all legs and not much else anybody'd look at—could hope to compete with a two-year-old Munchkin like Preston. Anyway, I don't *want* to compete. I mean, why would I want anybody going goo-goo over me? It'd make me vomit.

Oh, I don't know what's the matter with me. I'm going to bed.

4

I haven't written in this book for ages. Well, three weeks. It isn't that nothing's been happening. It's that I haven't had time to write about it. There's so much to *do* at the end of school, with exams and the Final Assembly and having to make up a health test I missed way back in April and forgot all about. And of course the Rose Festival going on in Portland, which keeps taking your mind off studying. And last weekend it turned really warm, warm enough to go swimming in the neighborhood pool. We all went, Saturday and Sunday both. Preston loved it. He was like a little fish, splashing and splashing so that he nearly drowned whichever one of us was holding him stomach-down, in a sort of swimming position. Sometimes he practically drowned himself, though he never seemed to care.

But today it's all overcast again and you need a jacket. Typical Oregon June weather—though for a wonder it didn't rain on the Grand Floral Parade this year.

So now school's out and it's just plain Monday and all of a sudden I've got more time than I know what to do with. It's always this way at the beginning of the summer. Here's all this freedom you've been looking forward to, and you can't think what it was you needed it for.

Well, for one thing I can catch this book up on "The Kelsey Mystery," as Alison calls it. I did finally tell her about the Grand Coulee story, though I probably shouldn't have. She gets so carried away. I only told her because I was irritated at Kelsey, and at Daddy too, and Alison was around, handy to explode to.

I started getting irritated quite a while back because of one of those dumb, pointless things Kelsey does when you're least expecting it. It was a week ago last Thursday. I remember because on Wednesday the Navy ships sailed into Portland harbor for the Rose Festival, and the next afternoon Daddy took us all downtown to go aboard one. Daddy picked me up at school to save bus-riding time, and waited in the car while I ran into the house to hurry the others. Kelsey was just getting Preston up from his nap. The minute I came in I could hear him laughing, upstairs in his little room, and Kelsey talking away to him the easy, cozy way she does when the two of them are alone. She never does it when anybody else is around. She kind of clams up and puts herself in the background, as if she's shy about letting us see she's crazy about him. Which is crazy, itself, isn't it? I mean, why wouldn't she be?

Well, anyway, I dumped my books and ran upstairs to get in on the fun, and I guess they were making too much racket to hear me, though I wasn't *trying* to sneak up on anybody. As I was coming along the hall Kelsey was blowing on his bare feet—I could tell by the way he was giggling, because he just loves that—and then trying to get his socks on, saying, "Hold still, Bitsy. Bitsy! Hold *still*!" It's always like trying to get socks on an eel. When I stepped into the room she was reaching for a sock he'd managed to kick off, telling him to cut it out, and still calling him "Bitsy," which I'd never heard before. I scooped up the sock on my way in, and grabbed his ankles for her.

Well, I startled her to death, though I didn't mean to, but it's so *easy* to startle Kelsey. She jumped and sort of shrieked and then laughed at herself of course, only pretty breathlessly and not as if she felt like laughing, and her freckles showed plain for a minute.

I said, "I'm sorry! Didn't you hear me come home?"

"No. Not a sound."

"Well, I banged the door, and ran up the stairs—" I was beginning to feel like it was my fault, and it wasn't. I quit apologizing and patted the soles of Preston's bare feet together. "Old Bitsy here was making too much noise, that's the trouble. Is that his nickname?"

She took one foot and wrestled a sock on, saying, "There you go! Now the other one!" just as if she hadn't heard me, or didn't realize it was a question.

So I asked again, "Is Bitsy a new nickname?"

Kelsey just murmured, "Hmm? Oh. No. An old one. I was just . . ." She got real busy with the other sock.

I said, "I like it. Hiya, Bitsy! Hey, Bitsy, look at me. I'm gonna put your shoe on!"

He did look at me, and grinned and grabbed for the shoe. You could tell he knew that "Bitsy" meant him. But Kelsey said, "Don't call him that." Her voice went real sharp all of a sudden.

It surprised me, and I said, "Why not? I think it just suits him. Doesn't it, Bitsy-boy?" I was trying to kind of joke my way past it, still wrestling with the shoe. I couldn't believe she was actually objecting.

But she was. "It's just a name we used to—*I* used to call him. When he was a baby. He's getting too old for it."

"Too *old* for it?" I said. I guess I stared at her.

"He'll hate it when he starts in school. I'm trying to quit saying it. It's hard to break habits. I'd rather you didn't form one."

Her face had tightened up, same as her voice, and her freckles were plain again. She absolutely meant it, and I could see no sense in it at all. So when he starts in school, okay— we'll quit. Though lots of kids have baby nicknames that last through kindergarten. I used to know a boy we all called Peter Cottontail till we were in second grade. That *is* too old. But two and a half?

Oh, well, she meant it. So I shut up. But it kind of made the jaunt downtown to go through the Navy destroyer not all that much fun.

I mean, it kind of hurt my feelings. I think she just doesn't want *me* using *her* private pet name for Preston. Well, I'm going to call him Bitsy whenever I want to—when she can't hear me.

And then on Saturday—it was the day of the Grand Floral Parade and I was going into Portland for it, with Alison and her mom—that very Saturday Daddy went on one of his all-day trips, and took Kelsey and Preston with him. He didn't even *ask* me.

When I pointed this out to him, kind of loud, I guess—I mean, he just sprang it on me without warning at breakfast— he said, "But aren't you going to the parade? I thought you had your day all planned!"

Well, I had. And maybe if he *had* asked me I'd have said no, I'd rather watch the parade than go on any old business trip. Especially if it wasn't going to be just him and me, the way it used to be. But at least he could've *asked*.

So after that I thought the parade probably wouldn't be so great, either. But before long I got in a better mood. You can't help it when you're watching float after float go by with these squillions of fresh flowers piled up in wonderful designs like ships and chariots and flags and I don't know what all, and then the royal float with the Queen of Rosaria and the princesses from all the high schools, wearing beautiful, fabulous dresses and waving to everybody. Well, you just can't watch all that, especially with Alison squealing in your ear, and still keep sulking.

I've never been much of a one for sulking, anyway. I'd rather just say, *it's over, forget it*, and start thinking about something else. And I can see—now—why Daddy figured I wouldn't want to go anywhere on Rose Parade day. He didn't mean any harm. But I can't quit having this little sore spot, like a toothache that's still there, because he didn't even *ask* me.

Well, so there was that. And then last Wednesday—it was a half-day, the last day of school—Alison came home with me and after lunch we fooled around up in my room awhile, just acting silly and feeling *free*. Then it quit looking like it was going to pour any minute, so we took a walk, and by the time we got home we'd decided *we* were going to cook dinner. Kelsey said okay, and Alison phoned her mom, but then we discovered there was no spaghetti, which is about all we know how to cook, so we put on our jackets again to walk to the 7-Eleven. Daddy came in the door just as we were starting out.

And of course he asked, "Where are you going?"

So of course *I* said, "Out of your life, forever!" and he said, "I'd kill to stop you!" and I yelled, "You mean—?" and he said, "I mean your lover, Richard!"

Well, Alison was just grinning and waiting—she must've heard those lines a hundred times—but I suddenly realized Kelsey was standing in the kitchen doorway staring at us as if we'd turned bright green. I guess it was the first time the routine's been triggered since she's been around.

She said, "What are you *talking* about?" in this halfway scared voice, and of course Daddy laughed and went over and hugged her and began to tell her all about it. Of course. Naturally. So now *that's* not just ours any longer, either.

I didn't wait around to hear it all explained away and ruined. I just said, "Let's go," and pulled Alison on outside and down the walk.

She asked, "What's the matter?"

I said, "Nothing." But I couldn't help adding, "I just wish Daddy wouldn't tell Kelsey all our *private* things."

"That's private? That act? I've heard you do that all my life, practically."

"Well, I know you have! You're different. You were around when it started. You knew Margo!"

I could feel Alison studying me, sideways, and I could tell she was going to start analyzing my character in a minute. Or maybe sticking up for Kelsey. So that's when I told her about Kelsey and Grand Coulee.

She didn't believe the story any more than I do. But she liked it. In fact she loved it. I might have known. She wants to put it all into our mystery book plot—all the odd things Kelsey does, and her jumpiness, and Grand Coulee, and everything.

But I wouldn't do it. I mean, lots of times I get annoyed

with Kelsey, but other times I think she's really scared of something. If she is, we oughtn't to put her into our dumb mystery plot and kind of make fun of her.

This morning I made six dozen cookies and it only took two hours. There just doesn't seem to be enough to *do* in summer. I wish you didn't have to be fifteen to get a job. I bet I could do whatever a fifteen-year-old can do. If you're twelve, the only job they'll let you take is picking berries and beans and things. And I don't have a way to get to the fields.

Maybe I'll call Alison and see if she wants to walk over to the mall. We could take Preston and get him an ice-cream cone. *If* Kelsey will let us.

Evening

Kelsey wouldn't let Preston go with us. Well, the truth is he didn't want to. She was sort of hesitating, and I held out my arms to him, and asked, "Wanna go buggy-ride?"—which is what we call going in his stroller—and he just kind of looked at me and then turned away and hung on to Kelsey's jeans and rubbed his face against her.

She said, "I don't think he feels very good today. He's been awful fussy."

Well, he had—and he did pick up a little cold somewhere, maybe at the swimming pool last weekend. But I said, "It's warm out. This'll cheer him up. Come on, Preston—wanna ice-cream cone?"

He just burrowed further into Kelsey and then tried to climb up her. She picked him up and he put his head down on her shoulder and gave me a look that said *get lost, Juniper* as plain as day.

Kelsey said, "I think he'd better stay home." And I nodded and smiled real hard. It *felt* too hard, anyway. Maybe it looked all right.

I know it was dumb to let it get to me. After all, it's natural for him to like his own mother better than anybody, especially me, especially when he's feeling lousy. But coming on top of everything else, for a minute I just could hardly stand it. *Everybody* likes Kelsey better than me.

I guess that's not really so. It just feels like it.

Alison and I went to the mall anyway, and she found some white shorts she thinks her mom will buy her. I need a new swimsuit, but I didn't look for one. I wasn't in the mood.

FRIDAY, JUNE 21

Kelsey dyes her hair. I found the bottle in her bathroom wastebasket this morning when we were sorting the trash for recycling. I only stopped and peered at the label because I didn't know what it was, but she went all pink around the cheekbones and grabbed it to put in the glass-collecting carton, and began explaining right away, as if she was ashamed of it, that she touched up her hair because she was going gray.

I said, "You *are?* Already?"

"I know it's early. I—that is, prematurely gray hair runs in my family. My father was nearly white before he was thirty."

"Really?" I was kind of fascinated. "My fifth grade teacher had almost white hair, and she was pretty young, too, but older than you. I always thought it looked great. So *different*."

Kelsey smiled a sort of tight smile and shook her head, and said it made her look old, and she didn't want to look old until she *was* old. Then she picked up the carton and went on downstairs. I still think silvery white hair would look just beautiful on her, with those brown eyes, and because she looks so extra young in the face.

I wish I had brown eyes, like hers and Preston's—like Margo's—or really black ones like Alison's. They *show up* so much better than other colors. Except bright blue ones like this year's Rosaria queen has. In books the heroine mostly has either melting dark eyes or cornflower-blue ones. Or sapphire blue. Or turquoise blue. Sometimes the villainess has green ones like a black cat's. You never see any glamorous descriptions of hazel eyes, like mine.

I got wondering if I could think of any, so just now I took my hand mirror over to the window and really *examined* mine. I wonder why they're called "hazel." That's a kind of *nut*. Reddish brown. My eyes are sort of olive-green around the edges and lighter green toward the middle, with brown sprinkles. I don't see anything "hazel" about them. Or anything glamorous, either. They just look like eyes. Glass eyes, really, when they're staring into the mirror like that.

Oh, well.

SUNDAY, JUNE 23

Daddy took Kelsey to an old Douglas Fairbanks movie this afternoon down at the Arts Cinema, and I got to baby-sit Preston. It was fun to have him all to myself. I got him up after his nap, and got him dressed—after a lot of sock-throwing and giggling and all that. I'm glad we weren't in a hurry.

He's nearly over his cold now, just a little sniffly, and back in a good humor. When I was helping him blow his nose— or trying to get him to—he teased me by just staring up at me over the Kleenex and pretending he didn't know why I was holding it there. I kept saying, "Blow, Preston!" (and sometimes I said, "Blow, Bitsy!"), and finally I made my lips all rubbery and blew through them to make a nose-blowing sound, and that gave him the giggles. So then *he* blew through his lips and made the same bu-bu-bu-bub noise—and could I get him to blow his nose after that? Nothing doing. I finally just wiped it and took him out to the backyard. Daddy's fixed a little canvas bucket-swing for him out there, hung from one of the branches of the oak tree.

I pushed Preston in his swing till he got tired of it, then he mooched around the yard checking out the bug population, then he got bored again. So I asked, "Wanna dance?" and took both his hands and began to show him the foot-dance Margo used to do with me when I was little. It's just a sort of a heel-and-toe, then pick him up and twirl once, but he liked it fine. Whenever I stopped he'd say, "Wanna dan!" and we'd have to do it again. I finally ran out of steam, so I asked, "Wanna sing?" and started in on "Mary Had a Little Lamb," which was another of Margo's and my best numbers.

We sang together quite awhile—well, sort of together— me doing the singing with him coming in strong on the "lit-*tul* lamb" and sort of wavering all around the rest of it. He called it "Wanna sin!"—which always cracked me up, so *he* always cracked up, too, without having a clue why. His little shoulders just *shake* when he laughs hard. Sometimes he's so cute I just have to grab him up and swing him around and around and around.

When Kelsey and Daddy came home we were eating cookies and milk on the back steps, and practicing "Mary Had a Little Lamb" with our mouths full, and he was so busy getting in his "lit-*tuls*" that he hardly looked at Kelsey.

She put him to bed awhile ago, and when she came down she said, "Juniper, thanks for being so nice to Preston. He had a great time today. He really likes you!"

Which kind of made me feel guilty, I don't know why. All I was doing was playing with him the way Margo used to play with me. It isn't as though I was trying to get him to like me *better* than Kelsey. Or maybe I was.

TUESDAY, JUNE 25

I found out where Kelsey got all her information about dams and mechanics' jobs and living in trailers. There's a book on hydroelectric power in Daddy's bookcase, and there it all is, with pictures and everything. I spotted it this morning when I was trying to find something new to read. Maybe that's where she got the whole Grand Coulee idea.

I'd sure like to check up on that story. But how? Everybody's dead or in Australia. Or never existed. Maybe they did, though. Maybe they were all as real as I am. It's certainly *possible*. Only how would I find out?

"Dear Grand Coulee Dam: Did you ever have a mechanic working there named Albert Morgan, with prematurely gray hair? Love, Juniper."

Yeah, great.

I wish I weren't just twelve years old. There're so many things I don't know how to *do*.

Guess what. Kelsey actually let Alison and me take Preston to the mall. She didn't want to. But there's really *no reason* why she shouldn't. Everybody takes their little kids there in strollers; it's perfectly safe. And Alison and I are *dependable*, and she knows it.

Besides that, Preston was on our side. He kept saying, "Wanna go buggy-ride. Wanna go Juper. Wanna sin!" and she couldn't really hold out any longer.

So. I finally won one.

5

SATURDAY, JUNE 29

Daddy took Kelsey and Preston on a used-car-lot tour this morning—he's going to buy Kelsey some kind of wheels so she won't always have to wait for him to take her everywhere. But I hate used car lots, so I phoned Alison. She said, "Come on over, we're making freezer jam." So I jogged over there, and helped her and her mom hull about a ton of strawberries (and we ate about half a ton in the process).

I watched how her mom mixed the jam—it's real easy, you don't even have to cook it—and wrote down the recipe so I could maybe make some for us, if Kelsey says okay. I think homemade jam is way in the future on her cooking schedule. She's still working hard at Julia Child. I've got to admit it shows. Last night we had a kind of chicken stew called coq au vin, only you pronounce it "cocoa van," and it was dandy. There's a lot left for tonight.

Anyhow, after the jam was in the freezer, Alison's mom went off to do errands and Alison and I settled down in her room to work on our mystery plot. We might as well. We've got all summer to do nothing in.

"Let's plan it right, if we're really going to do it," I said.

"The way Elizabeth Kenilworth said."

"Okay. I've got my notes right here. *Now* aren't you glad I wrote it all down?" Alison rummaged around in the stuff on her floor—her room's as sloppy as mine—and finally found the notes tucked in her ring binder. "Okay. First thing we need is 'an unstable, unresolved situation.' Something Character A must keep concealed."

"Like a murder, does that mean? Or an unexploded bomb?"

"Being an illegal alien would fit, wouldn't it? We could go on with our beautiful, exotic high school girl."

"Oh, yeah. Betsy Ross."

"*Not* Betsy Ross! Sarah—uh—Hughes. She can be Character A. Her real name is Juanita Chavez. And—I know!" Alison exclaimed. "She's not only an illegal alien, she's a spy for the Mexican government!"

You have to keep hauling Alison back to earth. I said patiently, "How come the Mexican government wants to know stuff about a high school in Hillridge, Oregon?"

"Oh, I don't know! Yes, I do—the principal is really the head of a *different* spy ring. Of a rival political party that wants to throw out the people in power and restore the king."

"The king of *Mexico?*"

"Well, they had a king once, didn't they?"

We were both a little vague about it. I said, "I think he was a Frenchman. Napoleon's brother-in-law or somebody." For a minute we groped back into social studies, searching for Maximilian—*now* I remember his name—then gave up and settled for a native Mexican dictator.

We went on fooling around with it for a while. What the notes said we needed next was "an odd or puzzling happening noticed by Character B." We decided Character B was another high school girl, an ordinary American one, only Alison insisted on naming her Daniella Sasha Nicole—which sounds like a sort of United Nations and uses up three of the names Alison's already decided she's going to name her children when she has some. And she said the puzzling happening Daniella Sasha Nicole notices is Sarah-Juanita talking Spanish on the phone.

Well, I didn't think old Sarah-Juanita would talk Spanish on a public phone, not unless she's really stupid. So I asked, "Why not have her keep dodging questions about where she grew up?"

"Okay, that's better," said Alison, giving me a sidewise look.

"And then she suddenly comes out with a whole pulled-together story about it. And in the story, her father's dead."

"Sure, that's good!" Alison said. "That's so nobody will guess he's a spy!"

She went on expanding on that, but I went deaf for a minute because I had this feeling I'd just seen the tail of an idea go by. I lost it, though, and when I tuned in again Alison was saying, "and Daniella Sasha Nicole never believed the story anyway. Nobody believes it. Or would it be better if everybody *else* believes it? Yes! Everybody else believes it and they tell Daniella Sasha Nicole she's crazy—"

"But she knows she's not," I said, "because just a few days later she happens to see a book in the school library that has that very same story in it, practically word for word."

Alison stared at me and asked, "*Really?* Did you?" and we both knew we'd quit talking about our plot. I didn't really plan to say what I did. It just kind of came out when I opened my mouth.

It was too late to back off so I sort of laughed, as if it didn't matter anyway, and told her about the book I'd found on hydroelectric power and dams and everything. And then I told her something else—that one day last week Kelsey said "Jim"

47

instead of "Tim" when she meant Preston's father. It was one morning at breakfast, and Daddy was asking if she had a driver's license—thinking about getting her the car—and she said, "Oh, sure, Jim taught me to drive." He said, "Jim?"—because she'd never mentioned any Jim—and she got real flustered and said, "Tim! Tim Blockman! How crazy!" and then she looked at Daddy and said, "It's no wonder. I've truly forgotten him." And Daddy reached out his hand and squeezed hers and smiled, and I quit watching.

I didn't tell Alison that part. Maybe I shouldn't be telling her any of this, but I can't help it. I mean, I need to talk about it. I need to make jokes about it and just keep it a silly game. And after all, forgetting the name of somebody you've been *married* to is not only a joke but an "odd or puzzling happening," in my opinion. Just right for our plot.

So we went back to thinking up stuff for our book, only really we were trying to think of some explanation for all the real stuff going on at my house, and we sort of permanently dropped Sarah-Juanita and Daniella Sasha Nicole and the high school spy ring.

I can't say our ideas were any more sensible than they'd been before. Alison said what if Kelsey's a kleptomaniac and has a record wherever she comes from. I said she sure *was* concealing it, then. She doesn't even like to go shopping.

Then Alison said maybe Tim Blockman's name really was Jim, and Kelsey's concealing *that* for some reason.

"But then wouldn't she think up some name that didn't sound exactly *like* 'Jim'?" I objected. "Anyhow, *what* reason?"

"Well—maybe he's not really dead."

We eyed each other, sort of trying it out. I said, "Maybe *he's* a kleptomaniac. Or some kind of criminal. Maybe he's wanted by the police."

"Maybe she's trying to hide from him!" said Alison.

"Or hide *Preston* from him!" That gave me a nasty little shock, and I quit feeling like we were just joking. "Maybe— maybe she stole Preston and ran away because Tim—Jim— Blockman was mean to them—"

"Yes! And he said he'd kill her if she left him—"

This time we were *both* getting carried away. I hauled us firmly back to earth. "And now she's married to my father, so she's a bigamist too! No. Forget it. None of that's so. We've been watching too much TV."

Privately, I thought we'd been yakking too much about mysteries, too. It was curdling our brains. I decided I'd better go.

But I was still thinking while I walked back home, and the idea I'd just glimpsed the tail of came back to me. It was about Sarah-Juanita pretending her father was dead so nobody would guess he was a spy—that is, she was trying to *protect* him. What if Kelsey is trying to protect somebody? What if she isn't concealing something *she's* done, but something Tim Blockman's done—or her father's done? It's perfectly possible.

Something. But what? And why does she have to conceal it?

I know the answer to "why": Because the something is an unstable, unresolved situation—a bomb that might still go off. I don't know the answer to "what."

I'm not sure I want to find out.

SUNDAY, JUNE 30

The minute I woke up this morning I had a thought, and I wish I hadn't. It made me feel as if I'd stepped off a curb and found out it was the Grand Canyon.

49

It's about Kelsey's hair. About why she dyes it. What if it's not because it's turning gray, but just to *change* it? Maybe it's really light brown or something, instead of dark. Maybe it's blonde, even. And she dyes it to *disguise herself*, so nobody from her past will recognize her.

That was the thought I woke up with. And right away I had a worse one. If she dyes her hair so she won't look like herself, wouldn't she have changed her name, too? *I* would. Anybody would. So maybe she's not Kelsey Morgan Blockman at all, and never was. Maybe she's really—whoever. Sarah-Juanita.

I called Alison to tell her, so I wouldn't have to keep thinking about it all alone, but she wasn't home. Just as well. Kelsey came in the house from her weeding just as I was putting down the phone.

MONDAY, JULY 1

Daddy took Kelsey to get her car today while I kept Preston, and she came home driving it. It's just your basic thirdhand stripped-down Honda, but it's bright green and she just loves it. She says she's never had a car of her own before. I guess she always drove Tim's. Or Jim's. If there *was* a Tim or Jim.

Daddy changed Preston's little car seat from the Chevy into the Jolly Green Midget, which is what she calls it, and she took old Bitsy and me around a few blocks. It really is neat. Daddy wouldn't buy a car that didn't run okay. Nobody could fool *him*.

Three more years till I can even get my *learner's* permit. Oh, well.

I went down to the neighborhood pool for a swim about four o'clock, and there was Alison. So we sat on our towels awhile and I told her about the hair dye and Kelsey maybe changing her name. She says I ought to find a chance to go through Kelsey's wallet and look at the ID stuff. Her driver's license and Social Security card and all that would probably be in her real name.

I said I'd try, but I don't know. I'm not sure I can actually get myself to do it. I mean, it seems so *sneaky*.

TUESDAY, JULY 2

I'm teaching Preston to sing "Three Blind Mice." So far we can't get much farther than "See how they run" because he goes all out of control trying to manage "They all ran after the farmer's wife" and all that, way up in those high notes. He gets miles behind and his shoulders start shaking and we both end up giggling too hard to carry on.

Alison and I took him to the mall today. She got those white shorts she wanted, and I found a red-white-and-blue T-shirt on sale real cheap. It's just right for our picnic on the Fourth. We're going down to Riverside Park to eat, Daddy and Kelsey and Preston and I, and stay for the fireworks. I hope Preston can stay awake—but we're taking his down comforter and pillow just in case.

I'm making a list—just in my head, I mean—of "unstable, unresolved situations" Kelsey might be concealing—sort of unscary, harmless ones. *Not* ones like having to hide Preston from Tim Blockman. I don't want it to have anything to do with Preston. It's not a very long list yet, though.

Kelsey had a doctor's appointment today—just a regular checkup, she said, she's not sick or anything—and she let Alison and me take Preston down to the neighborhood pool while she was gone! I had no idea she'd say yes. I guess she really does trust me—with Preston, anyway.

It made me feel guilty. I mean, more guilty than I was feeling already. Because the other day I did go through her wallet. I don't think I would have if we hadn't taken Preston to the zoo that morning, in the Jolly Green Midget. It was Kelsey's idea. She's getting braver about taking him places, I think—look how she's relaxed about the mall. We didn't stay long in the regular zoo—Preston's too young for the lions and bears and things—I mean, mostly they just sit around like public buildings, so he gets bored. But he loved the petting zoo. So did I, to tell you the truth—that is, I did until a cute little fawn nearly ate my purse. They're so soft-looking, those deer, and so *scratchy* to touch. Preston sort of pulled his hand back. *He* liked the ducklings. Kelsey held one for him so he wouldn't squeeze it to death; and I stood and watched him petting it with his little fat fingers and looking all sort of starry-eyed, and thought about my list that won't come out unscary, and knew I *had* to find out where Kelsey comes from, and what's going on.

So on the way home, when Kelsey sent me into the Safeway with her wallet to get some stuff for lunch, I went through her ID.

Well, I might as well have stayed honest. She practically *hasn't* any. One driver's license—Oregon—dated January of this year, and one Social Security card. Both made out—

unmysteriously—to Kelsey Morgan Blockman. But the funny part is that there wasn't anything else. No credit cards, no insurance card, no library card even—no *junk*. I mean, it's *weird*. Lots of times, when Daddy and I used to go on car trips out of town, I cleaned out his wallet for him, just for something to do. And because it always *needed* it. He'd have a whole flock of people's business cards he didn't want, and year-old stubs from shoe repair shops and the cleaner's, and all sorts of stuff he just never had got rid of. *Besides* all the stuff he needed.

I don't know, maybe men cram their wallets fuller than women do. I don't even own one, so I don't know. Maybe Alison knows.

THURSDAY, JULY 11

Daddy's bought some new life insurance—because of Kelsey and Preston. He explained it all to me last night. The policy he had before, which had Margo and me as beneficiaries, or however you spell that, started being for me alone after Margo died, and he didn't want to change that. So he bought some more. Now he's got to pay two premiums, and he said it might pinch us all a little for a while. I said I wouldn't have minded going halves with the old insurance, but he said no, he couldn't feel it would be adequate for three.

"And all three of you must be looked after, *well* looked after, if anything should happen to me," he said.

"Oh, Daddy! What could happen to you? You aren't expecting to walk in front of a truck, are you?" I sounded cross and unreasonable. I could hear it myself. But Daddy never gets cross back at me.

He just said, "Of course not, Juni. But insurance is for problems you *don't* expect. Things do happen, whether we expect them or not."

Well, I know that, don't I? Think of Margo. He didn't need to remind me.

He looked at me a minute and said, "What's bothering you? It won't pinch us *hard*, I didn't mean that."

I said, "Oh, Daddy, I wouldn't care if it did, that isn't it. It's nothing." I went over and hugged him, and added, "Don't pay any attention to me." And I hope he doesn't. I don't know why I act that way sometimes. But I *hate* it when he talks about things happening to him.

This afternoon when Alison and I went over to the pool I told her about Kelsey's practically empty wallet.

She said, "That's *very* suspicious!"

"Suspicious?" I repeated. "Weird, yes. But I wouldn't exactly call it suspicious. Maybe she's just an ultraneat wallet keeper. Or my father's an ultraslobbish one. Is your mom's wallet fat or skinny?"

"*Bursting*," said Alison. "So is *my* father's. Isn't everybody's?"

I shrugged, since I've never noticed. I mean, it's not a thing you make a study of. I said, "Anyhow, Kelsey's driver's license and Social Security card are both in her usual name, so it must be her real one."

"Not necessarily!" Alison told me. "A person could get a driver's license in whatever name she made up, couldn't she? Or do they ask for your birth certificate or something?"

I shrugged again, and asked, "How do you get a Social Security number?"

This time we both shrugged. We're really totally ignorant.

"I'm going to find out," Alison said. "I'll ask my mom."

She phoned me a little while ago and told me her mom didn't know. "She can't even remember getting her Social Security number. She says she just always *had* one. And my dad got mine. She knows she had to take an Oregon driver's test when they came here from Minnesota, but she doesn't exactly remember getting the Minnesota license in the first place."

I guess she's totally ignorant, too. I can't ask Daddy. He might want to know why.

Alison also gave me a whole long list of stuff in her mom's wallet *besides* license and Social Security card. Three credit cards, four charge cards, two insurance cards, Triple A card, voter registration card, telephone charge card, a dentist's appointment card for last December, three shoe clerks' business cards—plus membership cards in the historical society, the art museum, the Oregon Memorial Association, the Oregon Realtors Association, the Smithsonian Institution, the Portland and Hillridge libraries, the International Wizard of Oz Club, the Bat Conservation International, and the Save the Sheep Federation. I mean, it's worse than Daddy's.

It's like people kind of collect all this stuff in their wallets just by living. Like oak trees collect moss.

Kelsey's nearly empty one *does* begin to seem sort of suspicious. It's as if she hadn't really been alive until last January. At least, as if a person named Kelsey Morgan Blockman hadn't. So where does that leave Preston "Bitsy" Blockman, I wonder?

Later

I forgot to mention something kind of funny. Today at the pool we saw a man—a real tall, real blond man—that both Alison and I are pretty sure we saw the other day at the mall.

55

He wasn't *at* the pool exactly, in fact he was halfway across the little park. Just sitting on a bench. And the funny part is that at the mall he was sitting on a bench, too, just about that far away—just far enough so we couldn't really tell what he looks like. And what's even funnier is that both times he was watching us. At least it seemed like it. And when we noticed him he got up real fast and walked away. Both times.

I said, "Is he following us, or what?"

And Alison said, "Hey, *sure* he is! It's Character C!" I couldn't remember about Character C, but Alison did. " 'Some unexpected occurrence or a new character (C) enters the picture and changes it for everybody.' " I think she knows Elizabeth Kenilworth's whole outline by heart.

But I doubt if our tall blond man is going to enter any picture we're in. He's more likely a coincidence, and you're not supposed to have those in your plot.

6

It's really summer around here by this time. It makes Preston fussy—he doesn't like heat. He woke up early from his nap today, all cross and grumpy, so I told Kelsey he could go with Alison and me to the mall—we were going mostly to cool off in the air-conditioning, ourselves. She was in the middle of cleaning the kitchen and was glad not to have him on her hands, I think. Anyway, we put his little sun-hat on him and took him along.

And guess what. We saw that tall blond man again. Only I think he's a boy—just extra lanky. He was closer this time, and not sitting on a bench, but standing with his back to us, looking in a shop window—I thought—but then I saw it was a *baby-clothes* shop. And when I looked to see what he found so fascinating, I realized I was looking right at *him*—and he at me. There was a mirror behind the display. He was staring straight at me. The next second he realized it, too, and turned and loped off down the mall as if something was after him.

I said, "Hey, Alison?" and she said, "I saw!" We gaped at each other a minute, and I guess we were both wondering whether this was really very funny or not. Funny-peculiar, maybe. Not funny-ha-ha.

Then Alison said, "Is he a man, though? Or a kid?"

"Kid." I couldn't tell much about how old he was, in the mirror like that. But he didn't look *jelled* enough, somehow, to be a man. I just flipped out my hands, and said, "Oh, well. It's a cinch he's not going to bother us. He acts like he's scared to get within yelling distance."

"His plans are not complete yet," Alison told me in her creepiest voice. Then Preston began pointing at the Orange Julius place and repeating, "Ice cream, ice cream," like a little high-pitched buzz saw, and we forgot about Character C.

It was after we'd finished our ice cream that the funny-ha-ha thing happened. There's a shoe repair place on Grover Brothers' third floor, and last week I left my practically new white sandals because the buckle had come off already. So today we went up to get them. It's easy enough to take a little stroller like Preston's on the escalator; you just roll its front wheels on and support the back wheels until you get to the top and can roll it off again—or else Alison gets on first to support the front wheels, if we're going down. She always stands on the step in front and me on the one behind, so we can stop anything going wrong.

Well, I got my shoes, told the man "no sack" so I wouldn't have to recycle it, and just tucked the unwrapped sandals into the stroller with Preston, and we started down. About halfway between the third and second floors there was this woman on the other escalator, going up. Just an ordinary woman—I only noticed her because it seemed to me she was staring right at those sandals, with this startled expression on her face. And all of a sudden she gave this gasp and cried, "Robbers!"

Can you believe it? "Robbers!" I guess she thought I *stole* the shoes—because they weren't wrapped. Well, they do still look new. I had the repair receipt in my purse, and I would've said so, only it struck me funny to be called a robber and I started giggling. Anyway, Preston pulled off his sun-hat just then and I had to grab it quick before he could throw it off the escalator, which he can do like lightning. And by the time I looked over my shoulder for the woman, she'd got to the top and was gone.

Alison was staring after her, looking confused and asking me what she'd said, but at that point we reached the bottom and had to pay attention to getting the stroller off the escalator.

When we were clear I said, "She thought we were shoplifters! She said 'robbers'! For all I know she'll run right around to the down side and come after us!" I was still giggling, but embarrassed too. I mean, I don't want people to think I'm *stealing* something.

"Maybe she's a store detective," Alison said.

"Or maybe just works here." We were standing there at the bottom of the escalator looking up, halfway expecting the woman to appear at full speed and try to arrest us or something. But only an old man and a little boy came down, so we went on down to the mall level, still watching for her and feeling unfinished about it. I mean, I wanted to show her my receipt. But neither of us had really noticed what she looked like, though we both noticed a red blouse or jacket. All I remembered distinctly was startled dark eyes and sort of heavy eyebrows.

Anyway, she never showed up, so we went on home, arguing about "robbers." "She should've said 'thieves' or 'burglars,'" Alison insisted. "Robbers are *armed*. They have *guns*."

"Well, burglars don't work in broad daylight in shopping malls. She should've said 'shoplifters.'"

" 'Thieves' is shorter, when you're yelling."

I said, "Well, I'm none of them and I've got a receipt to prove it"; and we let it go at that, and pretty soon Alison turned off at her corner.

Preston was all hot again when we got home (so was I), so Kelsey gave him a nice cool bath and now she's reading him his duckling book Daddy brought home the other night. I think I'll stroll down to the pool and take a dip before time to set the table.

Later

This is *weird*. I can't believe it. While we were having dinner I told Daddy and Kelsey what happened today—about the woman on the escalator—just to say something, tell a funny story. I thought they'd *laugh*. Well, Daddy did—threw back his head and guffawed. But Kelsey turned as white as this paper, and stared at me as if I'd just announced the end of the world.

I couldn't imagine why. I said, "It was okay, really. I had my receipt." She didn't answer—shook her head about an inch each way but otherwise didn't move. It scared me, the way she was looking, and I said, "Kelsey? Are you okay?"

She mumbled something and tried to smile, and turned around to the high chair, pretending to wipe Preston's mouth, but Daddy had seen her face, too, and quit laughing.

He got up fast and went to her, asking if she felt all right and did she want to lie down or anything.

She said, "No, no. Of course not. I'm fine. *Really*, Charley, I'm okay."

But all this time Preston was sort of fending her off, because he was trying to eat and she kept leaning over him dabbing at his mouth so she could keep her back to us; and pretty soon he let out a frustrated sort of screech, which I couldn't really blame him for, and she had to give up and face us. She wasn't quite so ghastly-looking by then, but her freckles still showed like sprinkles of cinnamon on paper, and her eyes seemed too big.

Daddy said firmly, "Come on. You're going to lie down a while. D'you feel nauseated or anything?"

She started to say no again, I'm sure of it, but she changed her mind and said, "Just a little. Go ahead and eat your dinner. I'll just—" She got up and headed for the stairs.

We both watched her go. Then I half whispered to Daddy, "I'm *sorry!* I was only trying to—I mean, I thought it was *funny.*"

"It *was* funny, Juni. It wasn't what you said, this is nothing to do with that. Sure 'nuff." He ruffled my hair and smiled at me. "She's just not feeling quite top-notch lately."

I got this horrible, slow *sinking* inside me for a minute. I mean, Margo had just not been feeling quite top-notch that awful day, four—nearly five—years ago now. It was exactly what Daddy had said then, too. Just a little backache. A little fever. They'd make her better in the hospital. But it was meningitis. And three days later she was gone forever, from both of us.

I said, "Is Kelsey going to the hospital?" in this dumb voice that sounded like I was standing in a cave or something.

Daddy stared at me a second and then came around to my chair and gave me a bear hug. "No! Put it out of your mind, Juni! Kelsey's perfectly all right." He looked straight in my eyes until I knew I could believe him, then he rubbed his beard against my ear the way he used to when I was a little kid. "The fact is, she's going to have a baby."

"A baby!" I went straight from being scared to being flabbergasted. I don't know why—it's not unheard of, when people get married. But I just couldn't seem to take it in. A baby—Daddy's and Kelsey's—a brand-new person, right here in this house. My little half sister or half brother. I finally said, "When?"

"Not till way next winter. We weren't going to say anything yet, but I don't want you worrying. It explains a lot of things, you see? Just don't mention it till she's ready." He went back to sit down. "Let's finish dinner. Okay by you, Preston?"

Well, Preston hadn't really let anything interrupt him. He *had* finished, and was beginning to decorate his high chair tray, and the floor, with little dabs of leftover carrots, which yanked me back to the present in a hurry. Getting him and the floor wiped up helped me settle down inside, and trying to picture him becoming a *big* brother, next winter, to some little scrap of a baby, got me clear over being scared. It wasn't really me I'd got scared for anyway, it was Daddy. I just couldn't stand the idea of the same thing happening to him for the *second* time. Or to Preston even once.

Well, it's not going to. Kelsey's okay. She came downstairs even before Daddy and I had got all the stuff in the dishwasher. It was just one of her funny spells. And maybe the baby explains them all, even the one at dinner, but I can't see how. I thought people having babies just craved pickles and up-chucked in the early morning.

But what else *could* have brought this on? That woman on the escalator yelling "robbers"? I can't imagine it. Unless Kelsey thinks I'm really a shoplifter.

Or—could *she* be a shoplifter?

I remember Alison had that idea once. No, she said "klepto-maniac." I guess it's the same, as far as the store is concerned.

Except I think a kleptomaniac's family usually always pays for what they take, so they won't go to jail. Where did I read that?

I better go see Alison tomorrow. We've got to talk.

SUNDAY, JULY 14

I called Alison first thing this morning and let the phone ring about eighteen times before I remembered she and her mom had gone to the coast. They were going to leave at the crack of dawn and stay *all day* and drive back tonight. Church and a family reunion some place near Cannon Beach, where her grandmother lives. So I can't see her till tomorrow. Oh, well. I'm going to help Daddy mow the lawn.

Later

I wish I had something *real* to do. Our yard's not big enough to keep two people busy for even an hour. And mowing's not complicated enough to get your mind off anything else. Like Preston having a little sister or brother next winter. Two tiny little kids in the house—it'll sort of make me one of the grown-ups. Except to the grown-ups, maybe. *They'll* still think of me as a kid—too young for this or that or the other—unless I do something kiddish, and then they'll tell me I'm a lot too old to pull a stunt like that, so cut it out.

I wonder how I'll think of myself? As the baby-sitter, maybe.

Now it's clouded up and beginning to drizzle, so no use going to the pool.

Daddy's working on accounts. Kelsey's putting Preston down for his nap. Alison's at the coast. And all I can do is *think*. And not just about the baby.

63

What I keep thinking about is coming in from the yard this morning to get a Coke and Kelsey—real casual, *extra* casual—asking what that woman yesterday looked like. The woman on the escalator.

I said, "I don't know. We couldn't remember, later."

She was fixing some salad for lunch, and didn't look around at me, just kind of laughed and said, "You must have noticed *something.*"

"Not really. Well, we both thought she had on a red blouse, or maybe jacket, but I thought she had black hair and Alison thought brown. And we couldn't decide if she had a purse—I got the idea she maybe worked in the store."

Kelsey said, "Oh! Maybe that—maybe so."

I waited, but she didn't go on, and I remembered something else and said, "She had kind of heavy eyebrows."

No answer. Kelsey was concentrating hard on the salad, bending over with her front hair practically covering her eyes. After a minute I went ahead and got my Coke and one for Daddy, and opened them, and put replacements into the refrigerator, and was about to start out when she said, "Of course, a lot of people do." It left me blank a second, and she added, "Have heavy eyebrows."

"Oh. Yeah, they do," I said, and waited some more, but she finished the salad then, and stuck it in the fridge and then started washing her hands and humming as if she was all through with the subject, and it wasn't making her nervous at all.

Oh, no. Not much it isn't. Margo could have played that whole scene and convinced me she was just making idle conversation. But Kelsey is *no good* at acting. She's still worrying her head off about that woman. And it's the *woman herself,* not the shoplifting part, that's on her mind.

I wonder why. Just a stranger on an escalator wearing a red jacket. With heavy eyebrows. Maybe *she's* Character C.

I'm sure tired of *thinking*. I wish I had a job.

Lots later—after midnight

She thinks she knows her. That's the only answer. She thinks that woman is somebody from her other life—before last January—before Kelsey Morgan Blockman started having some I.D. and being alive.

But why would a woman from Kelsey's other life be gawking at my sandals, and why would she say "robbers"? That's such a dumb thing to yell at somebody.

Maybe she wasn't looking at my sandals. All I'm really sure of is—she was staring at the stroller. So what if she was looking at *Preston*?

Then what if she didn't say "robbers" at all, just something that sounded like it?

Like—what if she said "Robert"?

7

Alison and I have been *haunting* the mall. Without Preston, unfortunately. Kelsey clamped down again on our taking him along—the very next day after I told the "robbers" story. He got too hot that day, she says. It isn't good for him to get hot like that. Well, today it happens to be a fearsome seventy-three degrees out, with a nice cool breeze, but never mind. No mall for Preston, probably from now on.

She can't risk that woman being there again and spotting him. Which is exactly what *we want*—so we can find out who the woman is and why she yelled "Robert!" If she did.

We'll just have to watch for her without him. For all we know, she'll never go into Grover Brothers' store again in her life. But that's the only place we know to look for her, so we go every day, and ride up and down the escalators, and keep our eyes peeled. To tell you the truth, it's getting pretty boring.

"Maybe she yelled 'robbers' after all," I told Alison today when we gave up and slouched over to the Orange Julius place for lunch. I was feeling kind of discouraged.

"Listen, I've got an idea," Alison said. Alison's always got an idea, especially when she thinks you're about to poop out on her.

66

"None of our ideas work," I said.

"This one will. Get Preston away by himself this afternoon and try calling him 'Robert'! See if he acts like it's his name."

"I already *did* that. Right after breakfast Monday morning. Before I even told you about my theory."

"How come you didn't say so?" Alison looked real hurt.

"Well, it didn't work, so what was the use? At first I thought it had. I took him out to his sandpile and got sort of behind him, and suddenly said, 'Robert,' and he looked around right away. But then I decided I'd better test it, so a minute later I got behind him and said, 'Johnnie.' Well, he looked around *again*. Then I tried 'Mickey' and 'Hey, you,' but he looked around whatever I called him. Of course by then he thought it was a real funny new kind of game."

"Oh," said Alison. We drank Orange Juliuses and thought awhile, staring past each other's shoulder. Finally Alison said, "Who could she be, that woman? If she said 'Robert' she *recognized* Preston."

"Somebody who knew him before. Who knew Kelsey before."

"She's bound to be from out of town, then. So maybe she's already gone back, and that's why we can't find her."

"Unless she's stuck around in hopes of seeing Preston again," I said. "But if she wanted to see him again why didn't she rush right down the escalator after us? We were hanging around down there in plain sight—but she just took off somewhere. That doesn't fit at all." The whole thing was making me cross.

"Maybe she was too shocked. Maybe she fainted or something, and couldn't follow us!"

"Come on. Why would just seeing Preston make her faint?"

"Well ..." Alison said slowly, "suppose she's his real

mother. Suppose Kelsey stole him from her. I've heard of people doing that—people who want babies real bad and finally just *take* one."

I thought about it, but not long. "She was too old to be Preston's mother. She looked older than Daddy."

"Well, maybe his real mother is somebody else, but this woman *knows* her—and knows her little boy was stolen."

"That's possible," I said, and then I knew it wasn't. "It's *not* possible. Preston looks so much like Kelsey he's practically a Xerox. He calls her 'Mama' and that's who she is—his mama. We're on the wrong track."

Alison nodded and gave a big sigh. "So maybe the woman didn't yell 'Robert' after all. Heck. It was such a neat theory. I guess she's not Character C."

"Well, listen, she might've recognized him for some other reason. Maybe—maybe she's a police officer or a detective or something, and recognized Preston because she'd seen him with Kelsey. Maybe she's a *store* detective, transferred to Oregon from wherever she worked before—"

"—wherever Kelsey comes from," Alison put in.

"Yeah! And Kelsey shoplifted something there, or maybe a lot of things, and fled to Oregon to evade capture and—"

I heard myself beginning to sound like a piece in the newspaper and wondered if I was just inventing our mystery plot again.

But Alison said, "That really is possible. It would explain everything. I wonder how we could check it?"

"Her clothes?" I said. I was just guessing. "Maybe they'd have out-of-town labels if she stole them."

"Even if she *didn't*!" Alison cried. She gave a little bounce, all excited again. "Why didn't we think of it before? I'll bet *something* she owns has a label from whatever store she got it at, in whatever town she came from! All you have to do is go through her closet."

Oh, that's all. First her wallet, now her closet. It's all very well for Alison—she doesn't have to do any of these rotten things, she just tells *me* to do them.

Of course, it's *my* stepmother we're investigating. It's my problem. So I guess I'll do it. Maybe tomorrow evening. Daddy and Kelsey are going out, and I'm baby-sitting.

FRIDAY NIGHT, JULY 19

There's not a single label in any of Kelsey's clothes. Even her sweaters and winter coat. Except in a couple of shirts she got just recently—and all they say is "100% cotton, wash separately, line-dry." And of course the Levi's label on her jeans. But no store labels. I think there used to be one in her coat, and she cut it out. There was a square place inside the right front that looked different from the stuff around it—like when you take a picture off the wall. She must have cut off all the labels there were.

I wish I hadn't found out. I mean, this makes it *real*. She's somebody else—and trying to hide it. Not that I didn't think so before, but I didn't know for *sure*. Or even quite believe it. I kept telling myself I was probably just making the whole thing up.

Daddy is telling himself it's all because she's having a baby—all her nerves and funny reactions. Well, I never heard that having a baby made you cut the labels out of your clothes.

Of course, he probably has no idea she's done that. He has no idea of a lot of things because they're not things you notice unless you're snooping—or because he's gone all day and isn't around when they happen, the way I am. Besides, he feels close to her, and trusts what she says without question. He's a very loyal, trusting person. I guess I'm not.

I can't decide if I ought to tell him about this. I bet he wouldn't see anything at all alarming in it—or even important. So Kelsey doesn't like labels. So what? They scratch your neck. Not the ones inside your coat, but never mind, he'd reason that away somehow. Or start *explaining* Kelsey to me again. Or worrying about *my* problem of adjusting. Or bawling me out for prying in Kelsey's closet.

I couldn't blame him if he did that. I'm not ever going to snoop around in anybody's personal belongings again. Let Alison do it if she wants to. I don't like the way it makes me feel.

WEDNESDAY, JULY 24

All *sorts* of things have happened. Where'll I start? With Monday afternoon, I guess, when Alison and I were on Mall Patrol. I really didn't want to do it anymore, I'm *sick* of the mall, but Alison's just like a mosquito for being persistent. A good thing, too. If we hadn't been there—right where we were, right *when* we were, and with *who*, I mean *whom*, we were . . .

I'd better start over. Monday afternoon, when we got to the mall, Alison peeled off to the Clock Shop to leave her mom's watch to be fixed, and I went on to Grover Brothers'. I was supposed to take the escalator up to Four, which is the top, watching all the way for that woman, and Alison would do her errand, then take the elevator and meet me up there. Then we'd both escalate down, looking carefully around each floor as we went.

70

Well, I was rising slowly from One to Two, peering around below me, and I caught sight of that tall blond kid again. I noticed him because he was practically running—toward the foot of my escalator. I got to the top about then and lost him, but on the way up to Three I kept an eye out, and sure enough, when I was almost there he stepped on at Two. He wasn't looking toward me or anything, and I decided it was *possible* he was just heading for men's suits, which is on Three, but I didn't believe it. It was beginning to make me mad. I mean, I was getting good and *tired* of him tagging me around.

So when I got to Four and spotted him getting on after some women down below me, I just walked behind a big display of curtains up at the top there and waited. There's nothing much on Four but offices, the home decoration department, and the beauty shop. I could peek through the curtain display, and I saw him get off, stand looking around a second, then start hurrying—it happened to be in my direction.

Well, I just stepped out in front of him and glared, and he stopped as if he'd run into a building. I said, "Quit following me around!"

He gave this big gulp that made his Adam's apple bob up and down. I saw he was a kid, all right, probably not much older than me, and staring at me like something in a trap.

I said, "Who are you, anyhow?"

He gulped again, cleared his throat, and said, "Peter John Eliot" in a voice that was just getting over being soprano.

Peter John Eliot. He said it as if it might mean something to me, and all of a sudden it did. I could feel my jaw drop—just the way it says in books. I said, *"Peter Cottontail?"*

He went so red his eyebrows looked almost white. "Pete," he told me in this sort of strangled voice.

"Sorry," I mumbled. I mean, if I hadn't been so surprised I

never would've been so tactless.

"Pete Eliot from second grade, Hillridge Elementary," he explained carefully. He was getting his vocal cords straightened out by now. "And you've got to be Juniper Webb."

"That's right."

"I wasn't sure. You've got so tall."

Other people can be tactless, too. I snapped, "Look who's talking," and waited for *him* to mumble, "Sorry," which he did, with another hair-whitening blush. "Is that why you've been following me around?" I demanded. "How come you didn't just walk right up and ask?"

"Not supposed to do that," Pete said.

"I wouldn't've panicked or anything," I told him. "Being followed everywhere bugged me lots worse."

Pete sighed and nodded. "I make lots of lousy decisions."

I decided to quit being mad at him. I could remember old Peter Cottontail—better than I remembered the rest of second grade. He was always doing something oddball, not quite how the teacher said to do it—but he was a nice kid. Kind of sobersides, with ears that stuck out. And a lot smarter than he looked. We used to be good buddies, way back then. "How come you suddenly show up in Hillridge?" I asked him. "I thought you moved away."

"We did. To Kansas City. Dad's just now wangled a transfer back to the Portland branch. You still live where you used to?"

"Yeah, on Madrona Lane."

"Then we're neighbors again. We found a house on Forest Road—about a block from where we used to live." He had the same slow, white grin, wide as a jack-o'-lantern's. "I'll be going to Hillridge Middle School next fall—same class as you."

72

"Well. Great." It suddenly occurred to me that when I'd last seen him—to talk to—Margo had still been alive and going strong. He knew her. He'd been in that second grade Christmas pageant she'd organized. He was the front half of Rudolph the Red Nosed Reindeer. I forget who the back half was, but I was a King of Orient—the shortest of the three. Things had really changed since then. *Everything.* I said abruptly, "My mother died."

All he said was, "Oh," but the way he looked when he said it told me a lot more—that it shocked him, that he didn't know what to say, that he was sorry, that he remembered being inside the front half of Rudolph the Reindeer and remembered *her*. Nobody, especially little kids, who ever knew Margo ever forgot her. I began to feel as if he'd never been away, that *he* hadn't changed, just got bigger, and that we were still the same old-shoe, sandpile buddies. I started telling him about Daddy getting married again, and Kelsey and Preston and all. Only I guess I shut up pretty suddenly about Kelsey, because he noticed.

"You don't like her?" he said.

"Oh, sure I do. I mean, she's real nice and everything."

"Only what?"

He hadn't got a bit less sharp since the second grade. I said, "Well, there's some things I don't understand yet. I'm working on it."

He nodded and dropped the subject, only it didn't stay dropped because the next thing he said was, "How come you ride up and down the escalators all the time?" Well, I didn't know how to answer that one. Fortunately, he went right on. "Is that your best friend, the girl who's always with you?"

"Yeah. Alison Fisher—don't you remember?" He shook his head, and then *I* remembered that Alison and her mom didn't move here till the summer before third grade.

Just about that very minute, I saw Alison coming toward us from the elevators, her eyes wide and her mouth dropping open when she spotted who I was standing right beside and talking to. I said, "Come on, I'd better introduce you."

We started toward her and met near the credit office, just across from the up escalator but a good half-block from the elevators, which are clear down by the beauty shop, the whole length of the fourth floor away. All this is important.

So I introduced them. Alison was taking him in, head to foot, with her eyes gleaming in her round black face. She glanced at me and said, "So. Does he say he can explain everything?"

"I'm doing my best," Pete said nervously. I guess he thought Alison might bawl him out, too. But she only laughed and I started telling her about the second grade, but something red caught my eye down by the beauty shop, and I focused on it and broke off with a sort of electric shock.

"Alison!" I practically screeched. "There she *is*."

"Who? Where?" cried Alison, whirling around right in my way as I was trying to dodge around her.

"Our woman! Quick! She's about to get on the elevator!" I nearly knocked Alison down trying to sprint past her, but before I could get up any speed somebody grabbed my arm and I did a sort of *tour-jeté*-type leaping turn like in ballet class and darn near landed on my nose. It was Pete, saying something urgent I didn't hear because I was indignantly telling him to LET GO, but then I realized he was saying, "*Escalator! Quicker!*"; and after one glance at the elevator—it was the middle one, and the doors were just closing behind the woman—I also realized he was right. So I quit fighting and sprinted for the escalator instead, Alison right beside me and Pete galumphing along behind.

We didn't just tamely ride down on the escalator, of course. We pounded down the steps as fast as we could manage without bowling over all the innocent bonafide shoppers trying to ride down too—edging real politely past old ladies and mothers with children, then leaping onward three steps at a time. Pete kept his neck craned to spot the elevators on each floor and gave us instant bulletins: "Middle car didn't stop on Three—going on past Two—"

And wouldn't you know, on the last lap from Two to One we came smack up behind a couple of broad-beamed, unhurried shoppers standing side by side and filling the whole stair, yakking away too hard even to hear me saying, "Excuse me." When one of them finally did, she simply gave me this drop-dead look over her shoulder and didn't move an inch. They even took their time stepping off at the bottom and moving away, still yakking.

By then the last person was leaving the middle elevator—a man with a briefcase. I couldn't see the woman anywhere. Pete suddenly said, "Red jacket?" Alison said, "Yes!" and Pete pointed toward the side exit doors, the ones that open directly outside to the parking area and the shelter where the special mall buses stop. I just glimpsed a red blob outside, beyond the glass doors—maybe our woman, maybe not—but we all started for the doors anyhow, without much hope because we were miles behind by that time and the main floor was crowded with people going every which way.

We finally got through the doors and outside, and there were all these millions of parked cars, and Alison said, "We'll never find her here!" But Pete, who seems to have more brains than the two of us together, pointed again. The woman was just getting on a bus. About twenty seconds later it drove off.

We stood in a row and watched it. Pete said—sort of sad but still trying—"It was a number 48."

We nodded. That one shuttles between Portland and some suburbs south of here. We'd narrowed our search to about two counties.

"At least she hasn't gone back out of town," Alison reminded me. "She's sticking around, the way we thought."

"Maybe she doesn't even live there anymore. Maybe she moved here," I said.

"She might've. We might find her yet."

Pete had been turning his head from one to the other of us, like watching a tennis match. Suddenly he said, "Would anybody like to tell me what this is all about?"

Alison and I both looked at him for a minute, then at each other. He'd been pretty darn helpful, when you thought about it. Without even knowing the score. Helpful and smart. By the time we broke eye contact, we'd decided.

"Okay," I said. "Let's get out of here and go someplace where we can talk."

We went to the park and sat under a tree, and I told him the whole Kelsey mystery, and how far we'd got investigating it, which wasn't far, and about the woman yelling "robbers" or maybe "Robert" and our various dumb theories, none of which would hold water and all of which sounded stupid when I tried to explain them to him. Of course I didn't give away the secret about the new baby.

He just listened, blinking now and then but not saying anything. When I'd finished he took a real deep breath and said, "Wow. I see why you want to find that woman."

"What d'you think?" Alison said. "Was she saying 'robbers' or 'Robert'?"

Pete just shrugged. After a minute he said, "You know what? You better go kind of careful. You better find out *all* about this before you go blowing the whistle on—on Mrs. Webb."

"It's okay, you can call her Kelsey, everybody does," I said. "Why have we got to be careful?"

Pete shifted sort of uncomfortably, folding both long legs up like jackknives and wrapping his long arms around them. "Might be dangerous," he said vaguely. Margo would've said he threw the line away—that's what actors call it when they speak an important line in a real casual voice, only making sure the audience gets it.

Well, I got the line, all right—so did Alison; she sort of came alert—but neither of us really got his point. She asked, "Dangerous for Kelsey, you mean?"

Pete said, "Dangerous for everybody." Without giving me a chance to ask why, which I was going to, he changed the subject. "I'm kind of interested in this Tim Blockman—or Jim, or whoever."

"He might not even be real," I reminded him.

"Yeah, well, even if he's not. Or even if he's dead. There's a lot we don't know about him."

"If he's dead, what's there to know?"

"Well—like did he drown or did she kill him?"

Alison and I both stared at him. I said—louder than I meant to—"You're crazy. Kelsey wouldn't *kill* anybody!"

"Not even to save her little kid's life? Or her own?"

"No! I mean—I don't know. But I can't even imagine—"

"It's awful hard to imagine somebody else's life," Pete said.

"Or what a person might do in a real bad situation. What you might do yourself, even."

I didn't know what to say, so I didn't say anything. Neither did Alison. I don't know what she was thinking, but I was trying to imagine some big bully yanking Preston around, hurting him, *trying* to hurt him. In two seconds I was so mad I was gritting my teeth and imagining myself grabbing up a poker or a lamp or something and just *smashing* it down on the bully's head, over and over, and screaming at him, and kicking him. I mean, it scared me, how I felt, and how *fast* I felt it.

I had to suck in a sudden big breath and sort of pull myself back to the nice quiet park. I noticed Alison was blinking hard and staring at Pete as if he'd opened a box of snakes. Maybe she'd been imagining somebody hurting her cousin Tracy's little boy, Sammy.

"So—okay," I said, trying to get my voice to sounding normal, only it didn't. "We proceed with caution. Or do we even—proceed? You think we ought to drop it?"

"Oh, hey, that's up to you. I didn't mean to butt in. You're not doing any harm, are you?" Pete acted real embarrassed. "I only meant—it might be serious, so watch out."

Well, I've always *felt* it might be serious. I know that's why I've tried so hard to laugh it off, inventing all that junk about Sarah-Juanita, mall patroling, trying to turn it into a sort of detective game. But until Pete said *did he drown or did she kill him*, I never thought how serious *serious* might be.

Neither Alison nor I were saying anything, and I guess it made Pete nervous, because he said, "It doesn't have to be *that*. It might not be anything your stepmom did at all. She might just've got caught in the middle of something she can't handle. Like maybe somebody's blackmailing her—for something her dad did, or her sister or somebody, that she can't tell about. Maybe she saw a crime committed and she's scared to testify. Maybe there's a big drug dealer in her family, and she wants to get shut of him, name and all."

It seemed to me everything he said got wilder and scarier. Blackmail? A drug czar in the family? Well, how do I know? Or maybe Pete just sees more TV movies than I do. I didn't say anything, though, and neither did Alison; we were just watching him like we'd forgotten we had tongues. So he said, "You could check on the drug thing, more or less. It would make you feel you were doing something."

I located my voice and said, "How?"

"Oh—just bring the subject up. Find a story in the paper about drug stuff. Front page is full of them. Read it aloud, say something about it. See how she reacts."

I told him that judging by her reaction to my escalator-woman story, a drug story would probably give her heart failure. He just said, "Not if drugs aren't the problem."

Well, I hope they aren't. Because I'm going to try that—if only to get it off my mind.

8

As soon as I got home from the park yesterday I hunted up the morning paper and found three drug-related stories without half trying. I boned up on one, and at dinner I dragged it into the conversation and repeated it almost word for word. It was about one of those late-night robberies of some little twenty-four-hour grocery—smash and run—only this time the owner, who'd been clubbed to the floor, stuck out his leg in time to trip the last robber out, and the guy crashed down all tangled up with the newspaper rack, and broke his arm. He was a high school kid—fifteen. The cops got the other two within half an hour. All stupid kids, all stoned on something.

Of course I was watching Kelsey, and she tensed up, all right, but I got the idea it was *me* she was reacting to—not the story but the fact that I'd told it. She gave me this odd, level look as if she knew I was aiming it at her.

It was Daddy who commented. "A happy ending," he said dryly.

"*Happy?*" I repeated. "One of those kids has got a broken arm and they'll all have *police* records now!"

"And with luck, a brand-new suspicion that there might be

better ways to get money. This way's going to cost them a packet in damages—worked out at minimum wage, not paid by their folks."

"It won't teach them anything," Kelsey almost snapped. "Not if they're on drugs. It won't stop them. They might as well go downtown and jump off the Fremont Bridge right now. Their lives'll just get worse. And worse. And worse."

"Honey!" said Daddy, staring at her. I was startled, too. I mean, I'd been waiting for one of her turning-white-or-red reactions, for something nervous and uneasy, not for this flat, hard voice. It hardly sounded like Kelsey's voice at all.

She said, "Well, it's true."

Daddy said, "There are plenty of recoveries. People turn themselves around all the time, and stay clean for years."

"Good luck to them," Kelsey said. "Everybody want ice cream? I've got vanilla and butterscotch ripple."

End of conversation.

I'm not sure what to make of it. I don't think anybody could sound so bitter—even about the drug problem—if they didn't know more about it than what you can read in the paper. On the other hand, it didn't make her nervous to talk about it, or scared, as it would have if a drug king were after her. She just made us a present of her opinion and slammed the door on the subject.

On me too. I guess she's begun to notice how often I bring up subjects that bother her. In one way it makes me feel guilty and sort of—I don't know—ashamed of myself. But why? I haven't done anything, have I? I mean, it's the very *first time* I ever did it on purpose. And I wouldn't *have* to if she didn't hide things. So in another way, it makes *me* stiffen up, too.

I wish we wouldn't—either one of us. I wish none of this

was happening. We liked each other at first. At least, I thought so. I think she'd be real nice—really neat—when you got to know her. I'd like to talk to her about the baby. But she doesn't even want me to know about that—she just won't let me in. I mean, here we've lived in the same house for nearly three months and I know just how she laughs and how her front hair flips around when she turns her head quick, and the little delicate moves she makes putting her contacts in, and what she likes for breakfast, and the way she carries Preston with one hip stuck out—and yet I don't know a thing about her underneath.

Well, I suppose I do now. One thing. She's antidrugs, and hard as nails about it. Okay.

But I wish we could go back to the wedding and start all different.

Later—after lunch

I'm going to phone Alison and go back to the mall. It's dawned on me—late, as usual—that when that woman headed for the elevator she might've just come out of the beauty shop. We ought to check there—to see if they know who she is.

FRIDAY, JULY 26

Alison and I didn't get far yesterday. When we got to the beauty shop I sort of backed off going in because I didn't know what to say. But Alison said, "Just tell them you thought you saw a friend of your mother's yesterday and ask if they remember a woman in a red jacket." I said, "If she was a friend of my mother's, wouldn't I know her name?" But that didn't stop Alison—nothing does. She just said, "An *old* friend. From long ago. You don't *remember* her name." She gave me a shove and I went in.

I mumbled all that to the first beauty operator I came to, and she stopped combing somebody out and frowned and said, "Red jacket? Lemme see. I don't think *I* worked on her."

Then the one at the next little dressing table said, "She might mean that sales rep," and the first one said, "Oh, did *she* have on a red jacket? I didn't notice," and the second one said, "Kind of orangy-red. She was talking to Edna." And the first one said, "Oh, yeah," and started combing again, and I asked, "Which one is Edna?" and the first operator said, "Edna's the boss. She's off till Monday. You come in Monday and ask her about it, okay?"

That was the best I could do, so I went out and reported to Alison.

"Sales rep?" she repeated, wrinkling her forehead at me.

I wrinkled mine back at her. "Somebody who sells supplies to the beauty shop, maybe? Shampoo and rollers and all that."

"Doesn't sound like our woman."

"No."

It was a letdown. We decided it *might* have been the general offices she came out of instead of the beauty shop—those offices are right next door.

"Come on, let's look," Alison said hopefully. "Because if it was, she'll be in there today—working."

She wasn't in there working. We went home.

FRIDAY, JULY 26, EVENING

Only two weeks till Alison leaves for Minneapolis and her

dad. We spent most of today together because she's going to be busy all tomorrow—orthodontist appointment and so on. I can't believe it's nearly August.

I'm going to be really stuck without her. Who'll I talk to about Kelsey? What if I discover all sorts of things and Alison's not here to get ideas and everything?

"You'll have Pete," she reminded me today when I was complaining about it on the way to the pool. "He gets ideas."

"Scary ones. Anyway, I might not run into him again. Now that he knows I'm who he thought I was, he won't be following me around to find out."

Alison looked as if she wanted to argue but couldn't think of anything convincing to say. "He seemed real interested yesterday," she said uncertainly. "In the mystery and all."

"This is today," I pointed out. "And where is he?" I knew that was unreasonable. But I wasn't in the mood to be talked out of being gloomy. I just said, "Pete's not you. It wouldn't be the same."

Alison knows better than to try to cheer me up when I want to be grouchy. She just said, "We've still got two weeks. Anyway, we'll write letters. And sometimes phone."

I thought of predicting that every time she phoned me from Minneapolis Kelsey would be sure to be right there in the room so we couldn't talk, but I decided I'd been cranky enough, so I told her we'd just have to solve our mystery in the next two weeks.

If we ever solve it at all.

SATURDAY, JULY 27, EVENING

I woke up this morning expecting a long, frustrating day with nothing to do and nobody to do it with. I was wrong. Pete turned up at our front door at 9:00 A.M. I'd only been up about five minutes and had on my oldest jeans and a wild-looking T-shirt that started out white but got washed with some red socks once. I was barefoot and hadn't combed my hair yet.

He took all this in in a split second and said, "I'll come back after breakfast."

I had to laugh, but I pulled him in and said he could have a piece of toast if he wouldn't hog all the marmalade. I guess he didn't actually duck as he stepped in the door but he sort of gave that impression—the way Daddy always does. Ceilings always seem lower when Daddy comes into a house.

Well, he met the whole family—I mean, Saturday mornings everybody's there, slopping around in old clothes. Daddy remembered him, and managed not to call him Peter Cottontail. Kelsey, in her robe, was frying bacon. She took him right in stride, just gave him that nice warm smile she has when she thinks this person isn't anybody to worry about, and asked how he likes his bacon. (He likes it crisp, like me.) I could tell she was a surprise to him, though he was careful not to stare. Maybe he was expecting some kind of witch or something.

We were eating toast when Daddy came in again with Preston riding on his shoulders, saying, "Here's another member of the family."

Pete stood up kind of self-consciously as if he was going to meet a celebrity—I don't think he's used to little kids. Preston just stared at him—at his ears, mostly. They still stick out, and they were turning bright red. Finally Pete reached up one big, bony hand, and after a minute Preston let go Daddy's hair with one of his, and let Pete shake it. Pete grinned as if he'd just got the Nobel Prize.

I left him watching Preston playing mud pies with his cereal, and ran upstairs to put on my good shorts and my sandals, and comb my hair. I changed my shirt too, but then changed back into the wild-looking one. I mean, I didn't want him to get the idea I was dressing *up*. When I came down he asked if I wanted to walk over to the park, so I said okay and we started out.

It was funny, we didn't know what to say for a while. I don't know why—it was real easy the other day, when we were bounding up and down Grover Brothers' escalators. He finally said, "I'm sure glad we moved back here," and I said, "Yeah, me too." Then I thought that sounded kind of—I don't know—so I said, "I mean, since you like it so much better and everything." And he said, "Yeah."

I was trying to think of a way to upgrade the conversation to at least average-bright, when he said, "I wanted to come over yesterday. My dad kept me too busy in the yard."

Well, that made me feel better, and then he asked where Alison was—and I told him—and if anything else had happened about the mystery—and I told him about the drug-story test and Kelsey's reaction, and about Alison and me going back to the beauty shop and how our escalator woman might be a sales rep.

"D'you suppose that means she lives somewhere around here after all?" I asked him.

"Might, if she works for a local outfit. Or she might travel for a supplier based somewhere else."

"And the somewhere else might be where Kelsey came from!" I suddenly felt more hopeful. "If we could just find *that* out—"

"What makes you think that's so important?" Pete asked suddenly. "So you get the name of a town. Then what?"

Good question. For a minute I didn't have an answer at all, though the feeling stayed strong that if we knew where she came from we'd be halfway home. "I don't know," I admitted finally. "It's just—well—she's taken such pains to *hide* it. That made-up story about Grand Coulee—the driver's license and Social Security card in a name that's probably just made-up too, and not even a *hint* of a background more than a year old. She never gets letters, she never mentions old friends. . . ."

"Yeah," Pete said. "I see what you mean. There's something there, wherever the place is. Something waiting to get her."

He did have the scariest way of putting things.

All at once Pete said, "I could probably find one thing out for you—how she could get a Social Security number to go with a phony name."

"You *could?* How?"

"Take the bus downtown to the Social Security office and ask 'em."

"Oh." For some reason, simple solutions never occur to me. "But would they tell you? Wouldn't they think *you* were planning to do it, and call a cop or something?"

"I'll say I'm writing a mystery novel," Pete said with his big, slow grin.

We just fooled around the rest of the morning, and I caught him up on kids he remembered, and he told me about Kansas City. We got a Coke at the 7-Eleven, then he had to go back to his yard work, and I came home to clean my room.

I think I like Pete just as well as I did in the second grade. Besides, he's taller than me. Lots.

MONDAY, JULY 29, EVENING

Well, we found out who our woman is. It took us *all day*, practically.

Alison and I got to the mall about as soon as it opened, and Pete met us on the fourth floor. We went right over to the beauty shop and I went in and asked for Edna. She was there—a kind of plumpish middle-aged woman with a cast in one eye and a tired expression. I gave my little speech about my mother's old friend whose name I'd forgotten—trying to look Edna straight in the eye so she'd see how trustworthy I was, which was hard because I couldn't tell which eye to look straight into.

She said, "Red jacket. Thursday, you say?" She sounded as if she didn't want to bother to remember that far back.

"And heavy eyebrows," I prodded encouragingly. I told her somebody had thought it might be the sales rep she'd talked to that day, and she said, "Oh. Blanche. She was here, yes. I believe she did have on a red jacket. And her eyebrows *definitely* need shaping," she added severely.

Of course I got all excited, and said, "Blanche who?"

"Hm? Oh, my goodness, I don't know her other name. 'Blanche' is all I ever heard. She works for Fairhair Products, over on the east side. Now, if you'll excuse me, honey, I've got quite a day ahead of me. . . ."

Well, I did, too, though I didn't know it yet. I said, "Thanks," and rushed out to tell Alison and Pete we had at least one name and a way to find out more. "Don't you think if we phoned Fairhair Products and asked for Blanche they'd probably know who we meant?" I said.

Alison said, "Why, sure!" and Pete said, "Maybe," adding that it depended on how big an outfit Fairhair Products was, and how many Blanches they had working for them.

"They couldn't have more than one," Alison told him. "*Nobody's* named Blanche. Come on, we'll phone at my house, my mom'll be at the office all day."

So we all went over to her apartment and settled down by the living room phone, which was immediately handed to *me*.

I grumbled, but it *is* my stepmom and my problem. So I said, "Okay, but you have to tell me what to say."

"Just ask to speak to Blanche," Alison said with this carefree shrug.

"What if they ask who's calling?"

"Tell 'em you're a relative just passing through town."

"Then when *she* comes on the phone I say I was just kidding? I better stick to the old-friend-of-my-mother story. After all, she really might be a friend of my *step*mother."

"Or an enemy," Pete said—of course. When I gave him a *look* he added, "Never mind, she can't bite you through the phone. Go ahead and dial."

I did. I knew I'd have to play it by ear anyhow. After a couple of rings, during which I could feel my heart going *bang, bang,* and sort of hoped nobody would answer, there was a receiver-lifting racket on the other end, and a smarmy female voice said, "Thank you for calling Fairhair Products, may I help you?" I said, "Uh, yes, could I speak to Blanche, please?" The voice asked, "Blanche Mitchell?" and I said, "Um, I think so. Have you got more than one Blanche working there?"

It was a mistake to be honest. A second too late, I realized Pete was flapping his hands and Alison was shaking her head and mouthing, "*No, no, no.*" Well, why hadn't *they* phoned, then?

The smarmy voice had gone chilly. It said, "Who's calling, please?" I gave her my old-friend-of-my-mother routine and she finally said, "I'll check." I rolled my eyes at my so-called friends while she went off somewhere, and Alison hissed, "You shouldn't have said that!" and I hissed back, "You didn't *say* I shouldn't!" and the voice came back to announce—smugly, I thought—that it was Blanche's day off.

I said, "Oh, then I'll phone her at home. Could you give me her number, please? Or just the address."

Well, I thought that was pretty quick thinking, but the voice took on ten more degrees of frost and said, "Sorry, I can't give out that sort of information."

I said desperately, "I just want to *talk* to her a minute. I'm not going to—"

"Sorry. It's *entirely* against company rules." She hung up.

Sorry, my eye. I hung up, too, and said, "She won't tell me. We could look in the phone book, though."

"Did she give you the last name?" Alison demanded.

"Mitchell." That didn't sound quite right. "Or was it Mitchum?"

"*Jun-i-purrrrr!*" Alison wailed.

Pete said, "Let's try Mitchell," and pulled the phone book onto his bony knees. Well, there wasn't a Blanche Mitchell listed in the Portland book. We tried Blanche Mitchum. Nothing. I said, "Try the suburbs—those pages with the dark edges." No luck. "Then maybe she's *Mrs.* Mitchell, and it's listed in her husband's name!" But Alison just wailed again and said, "If it is, we're sunk! There's dozens and dozens of Mitchells with dozens of initials. We'll never—"

"Haven't you got a county phone book?" Pete interrupted. Alison shut up in mid-wail and dug in the phone-table drawer, and we all huddled over the county book. At last—there it was. "B. Mitchell," in a town ten miles from where we sat. A man answered on the third ring, but when I asked him breathlessly if there was anybody named Blanche living there he said no, this was Bart Mitchell's residence.

I pushed the county book off my lap. It was only half as

thick as the Portland book but seemed to weigh a hundred pounds. Pete was already thumbing through the big book again. "We *looked* there," I reminded him crossly.

"Not for *initials* containing a B," he said. "Sometimes single women don't like to be listed under a female name."

I phoned every one he found. I wasn't even nervous by this time. And on the fifth try—P. B. Mitchell—*bingo*. The voice was a woman's, rather hard and abrupt. It said, "Yes, my name's Blanche. Paula Blanche. Who's calling?"

Well, *yipes*, who was? We hadn't made any plans at all for what I'd say if we actually got her. My heart began imitating a bongo drum again and I had to gasp for my next breath. I said, "Uh—well—this is—I'm the person you saw on the escalator at Grover Brothers' one day—it was maybe two weeks ago"—I stopped to swallow—"or more, and my friend was with me, and we had a stroller with a—a little boy in it, and some unwrapped sandals—we were going down and you were going up, and you . . . That is, I thought you sort of called out something to us, and—"

"Oh. I remember," she said. Well, thank goodness. I finally got a good deep breath from clear down in my innards and started to relax a little. But *then* she said, in this abrupt way she had, "What about it?"

"Well, I—I—I—" Oh, murder, what was I supposed to say now? I fell back on the truth. I managed a sort of garbled explanation about the sandals and the receipt and all, and how I'd first thought she'd said "robbers." No response. So I went on, "Then later I thought maybe you said 'Robert.'" I gave her a chance to say something, but she didn't. "And I wondered—which it was," I finished. I'd shot my bolt.

After what seemed about an hour and was probably ten seconds, she said, "Who is this? What's your name?"

Truth was no good this time. All I could think of was Pete's warning to be careful, to find out *all* about this before we went blowing any whistles on anybody. I said, "Marianne." I don't know where it came from, it just popped out.

"Marianne who?" she demanded.

"Jackson. I live on Northeast Stark." There must be a Jackson listed on Northeast Stark. Maybe even a Marianne.

"Tell me, Marianne, how did you get my name and telephone number?"

Well, I told her. I didn't know what else to do. But then I said again, "All I want to know is—if you said 'robbers' or 'Robert.' I—I made a bet with my friend."

There was quite a pause, then she said, "Okay, I'll settle your bet. But I want to tell you something first, Marianne. I don't like people tracking me down. It's an invasion of privacy. Especially when there's no good reason, and it's nothing to do with me."

"I'm sorry," I quavered.

"All right. I said 'Robert.' I thought that child was my nephew." She took a long breath that carried plainly over the wire. "But I was mistaken. Now, don't call me again."

The phone rattled in my ear.

"Wait, wait!" I yelled. "How do you know you were mistaken? How could you tell?"

But she had hung up.

9

I've been thinking and thinking—we all have, Alison and Pete and I—trying to get more out of that phone conversation than there really was in it. I wish Blanche had been the chatty type. Only maybe it wouldn't have helped a bit, just scattered more words for us to sift through and pick up and peer at and toss aside again, like people going through the confetti after a parade, hoping to spot at least one diamond.

What bugs me is the question she hung up on. One minute she was sure Preston was her nephew—sure enough to yell "Robert!" right out in public. Half a minute later she's off the escalator, out of sight, and never even tried to get another look at us. So what happened during that half-minute to make her certain she was wrong?

Another thing—this bugs us all, though it was Pete who brought it up, this morning when we were sitting in a row on a park bench, hashing it out once more. Why, if she thought Preston was her nephew, was she so dumbfounded?

"Maybe she hadn't seen him for a year or two," Alison offered.

"A year or two ago he'd have been wearing a bonnet and

waving a rattle," I pointed out. "She'd never have recognized him at all."

"Okay, then maybe he lives somewhere else and she was surprised to see him *here*."

"Surprised, maybe," Pete said. "But not *thunderstruck*. The way Juniper tells it, she was thunderstruck."

"She was!" I insisted. "As if she'd seen a ghost or something."

"Hey, could that be it?" Alison exclaimed. "Her nephew's dead! Preston looks like him, and just for a minute, before she really thought . . . Then of course she *did* think, and. . . ."

It was the best theory we could come up with. It does fit the facts. It explains all Blanche's reactions. But I don't believe it.

I keep thinking, what if Preston *is* her nephew, but she's got her own reasons for not admitting it—to me, to anybody—until she's ready. So when is she going to be ready? What is she hoping will happen? What is she *planning* to happen?

I don't like it. But it would explain a lot about the way she talked to me. The way she warned me off.

I haven't said a word about this to Pete and Alison. I don't want to get them started, they'd wind up scaring me to death. Because if Preston is Blanche's nephew, then Blanche is Kelsey's sister—or Tim Blockman's. Kelsey knows her. And goes white at the thought of her. Which leads us right back to *did he drown or did she kill him.*

I don't want to think any more about it.

WEDNESDAY, JULY 31

I just read yesterday's entry over and it sounds *paranoid.* I think Alison and Pete and I need to go see a silly movie or hike twenty miles for a picnic or clean out the garage or something. All we ever do lately is sit around inventing spooky fiction about some stranger we saw once on an escalator.

The plain truth is probably that Paula Blanche Mitchell is no relation to Preston or Kelsey or anybody else and she just made a dumb mistake.

FRIDAY, AUGUST 2

I'm going to baby-sit tonight while Daddy and Kelsey go out to dinner and a performance of *The Cherry Orchard*. Margo played Madame Ranevsky in that, the October after I turned eight. It was the last play she did. I don't really care if I ever see it in my life again. But we've been mentioning "the play" off and on the last few days and Preston's picked up on it, of course, and pipes, "Wanna go play" in a sort of anxious voice whenever he thinks about it. He can always tell if Kelsey's planning to go somewhere without him. He's a real mama's boy.

No, he isn't, though. That's funny. I never thought about it, but when Kelsey's just here, at home, he doesn't cling to her or tag around behind her or anything. It's only when she leaves him to go somewhere. Seems like that makes him feel unsafe or something. I wonder why. She never sneaks off without telling him—that's something you ought *never* to do to little kids, even if they throw tantrums trying to make you stay. That's what Margo always said. Seems to me Kelsey bends over backward to be truthful with Preston.

Anyhow, it'll be my job to calm him down when she and Daddy leave, and I've thought of a neat way to do it. I'm going to tell him *we're* going to have a play. That is, we are if I can

95

find that box of costumes and stuff Margo used to dress me up in. I guess it's still up in the storeroom somewhere. Unless Daddy threw it out. I don't think he would, without telling me.

Pete wandered by here this morning—well, more like lunchtime—and we walked over to the frozen yogurt place on Hill Road and bought two cones apiece and sat on the benches out in front to eat them. He said he went downtown to the Social Security place yesterday afternoon, and found out stuff.

"What'd they say?" I demanded.

"Well, it's real hard to get a Social Security number under an assumed name," he told me. "You've got to have a birth certificate or a certified copy. And you can't just go digging around in courthouse records and find one of somebody already dead, because they've got everything on computers and they check that name out nationwide. Your birth certificate has got to be of somebody living. And this living somebody very likely already *has* a Social Security number. So how're you gonna explain why *you're* applying for one under that name?"

"Okay. So far it sounds impossible."

"It is, if you do it that way. What you *can* do is apply for a replacement card. Tell 'em you lost the original—you've got to know there is one, issued to a live person, because they'll verify it. Then they need one piece of ID—driver's license is okay. This time they won't *accept* a birth certificate, don't ask me why."

I thought about it while trying to stay even with the frozen yogurt melting from my two cones at the same time. Pete's had got ahead of him while he was talking, and he was having to take big snapping bites to control the dripping.

"So what you mean is: If that card Kelsey's got in her wallet isn't truly her own, in her own real name, she's going around using somebody else's number? And the somebody whose card it *really* is, is using that number too?"

"Correct," Pete said, slurping.

"But how could she possibly hope to get away with that? I mean, forever? It's bound to be discovered."

"Just a matter of time," agreed Pete.

"So probably she didn't do it. The card's probably really hers, and Kelsey Morgan Blockman is probably her real name."

Pete shrugged while he chewed up the last of his second cone, and tried to wipe his big hands on the little bitty paper napkin they give you. "Might be, might not. She might have been willing to risk it. Depends how desperate she was to drop her own name."

In other words, yes and no. So that didn't get us any further. *Nothing* does.

Later—about ten o'clock, I guess

I got a shock tonight that I just can't get over. Not a shock, exactly. The creeps. I can't quit thinking about it and—if it's really so—I think I'm going to have to tell Daddy.

What happened was—well, nothing exactly *happened*. It was just what I *think* I saw—though I went in Preston's room just now and looked again and I couldn't really tell. Of course, I couldn't put the light on, because he's asleep. And the only flashlight I could find is dead. It'll be tomorrow before I can be sure.

Anyway. Early this evening after Daddy and Kelsey left, and I'd given Preston his dinner, I dug out the old costume box from the storeroom. It was still up there, all right—shoved underneath one of the lower back shelves so it was almost

97

invisible. I'll bet Daddy sort of hid it on purpose, so neither he nor I would keep coming across it accidentally and feeling as though we'd just bumped into Margo's ghost. It does bring her back, strong—you can practically see her standing there, bending over to open it, with her knees straight the way she always bent over, and her hair falling forward like shiny dark curtains on each side of her face. You can almost hear her— *Hey, Juniper, you want to be a big lady with a hat on, or a mean old witch, or King Lear with a long gray beard, or . . .*

It did give me a bad time, for a few minutes there, just looking at it. A big square cardboard box with "Margo Webb" stenciled faintly on the side, plus a straggly crayon decoration and label: "costumes" lettered by yours truly at about age six. As if we didn't know what was in it.

Well, I lugged it down to my room where it was still bright daylight—I guess it was about seven-thirty by then, and in summer around here it's not even dusk till after nine. My window's on the west, with low sun pouring in. So there was a really strong light.

I opened the box and began to take stuff out, watching to see what Preston might go for. He spotted a red velvet cape and began to tug on it, but it was so heavy he gave up. By then I'd come across the big-lady hat, and stuck it on his head, and of course he pulled it right off because he doesn't ever put up with hats very long. But I picked him up and went over to the mirror and put it on him again, and this time he got the idea and started grinning. That hat is the kind an old-time movie star might wear, black satin with a wispy sort of feather called an aigrette sticking right straight up from one side. He looked really funny in it.

After that he began to dig things out from under the red velvet cape and put them on *my* head—whether they were hats or not—so we ended up having a pretty good, silly time. I couldn't resist dressing him up in the Mustardseed costume from *A Midsummer Night's Dream*. It was too big for Preston, though it's child-sized, but he looked great in it anyway. It's nothing but two big balls of golden-yellow fuzzy stuff, one surrounding a little pair of underpants, the other covering a knitted cap. When Mustardseed comes onstage with Peaseblossom and the other fairies—he's the littlest, of course—he just looks like a couple of oversized dandelion clocks, with bits of bare little kid showing between and below. That costume's so cute nobody listens to the lines for a while—so Margo always said.

Anyhow. I held Preston up to the mirror to admire himself, which he did in an underwhelmed sort of way, as if he were humoring me and it wasn't going to last long. I guess he was tired of the costume game. He was tugging off the cap before I even set him down, dragging it backward so that his hair was all skinned back from his forehead.

And that's when I saw it. About an eighth of an inch of rusty-gold roots to his dark brown hair.

I *think* I saw it. The sun was streaming in, low and yellow itself, and gilding everything. That cap was all golden-yellow fuzz. And I only had a glimpse. The next second he had the cap off and his dark, curly mop was all over the place as it always is, and covering his hairline. I thought I *must* be mistaken—it was so hard to believe.

Naturally, I grabbed him right away and shoved the hair back and squinted at it, trying to make sure. Well, he wasn't having any. He squirmed and fussed at me, and batted at my hand and twisted away before I could really focus, and trotted off toward the bathroom saying, "Wanna go potty" in tones that showed he meant it. Well, we're encouraging that pretty hard around here lately, so I gave it priority—though I shoved his hair back again while he was sitting. No luck; I only annoyed him. The east light in the bathroom wasn't good enough and the electric one just cast shadows. By the time I took him back into my room the sun had dropped below the trees across the street and that yellow searchlight-effect was gone. I couldn't really be sure of any rusty-gold line—at least not in the two or three split-second chances I got before he fought me off, getting crankier all the time. I had to quit bugging him, and put him to bed.

So I still can't prove it. But I don't think it was the yellowish light, I don't think it was the yellow-fuzz cap, I don't think it was a mistake. And I *couldn't* make it up because I can hardly imagine it even now. In fact it gives me the *willies* to think of anybody actually doing that. But I'm ninety-nine percent sure Kelsey not only dyes her own hair, she dyes that baby's too.

SUNDAY, AUGUST 4

They were late getting home last night. I waited up. I just felt I *had* to talk to Daddy for a minute—which wasn't using my head, because naturally he said, "Talk? Hey, Juni, I'm half asleep. Tomorrow, okay?"

So then I figured they'd sleep late so I'd wake up real early, and get Preston up when he first peeped, and take a good look at that hairline in the morning sun. Well, *I* was the one who slept till eleven forty-five. When I came down, Kelsey was already fixing Preston's lunch, and after that comes his nap.

Daddy hadn't forgotten about the talk, though. He poked his head out of his little office room as I was wandering back upstairs, and asked if I wanted to drive to Salem with him.

100

"Old Bainbridge's main computer crashed just before quitting time yesterday and I told him I'd patch it up for him for Monday. Shouldn't take long."

Of course I jumped at the chance.

It wasn't any good, though. I mean, it was great to be alone with Daddy, just the two of us again, if I hadn't felt so uptight. He tried to help, when Alison was leaving, and how our mystery book was going—which almost *tongue-tied* me. I'd forgotten I ever even told him about that. What with everything, I had an awful time getting started really *talking*. About Preston's hair. You can't just *begin* on something like that, it would sound so weird. I knew he wouldn't believe me, and in broad daylight, driving down I-5 with everything looking perfectly normal and ordinary, I barely believed it myself. If I could've made *sure* before we started out it would've been so much better.

Well, anyway, I finally did just blurt it out.

Daddy gave me a quick, puzzled glance, turned the air-conditioning fan down a notch and in the sudden quiet said, "She *what?*"

"Dyes Preston's hair. I think. I'm almost sure."

Another bewildered glance, this time with a little laugh, almost embarrassed. "That's what I thought you said. Where'd you ever get such an idea, Juni?"

I told him. Exactly how it all happened.

"It was probably a trick of the light, all right," he said gently—very careful not to make me feel stupid, or sound revolted, which I know was how he felt, because I did, too. "I can see how the light might have fooled you. But I'm sure you're wrong."

I said, "I didn't think you'd believe me."

"But Juni," he said, still patient. "Come *on*. Can you see

101

Kelsey doing a thing like that? Taking a little two-year-old—taking *Preston*—and putting *gunk* on his hair? That fine, silky, beautiful . . . Let me put it this way. Can you see her putting lipstick on him? Or black mascara?"

"Of course not! But—"

"Well, it's the same thing, isn't it? Trying to improve on nature. Nobody in their right mind'd try to improve on a two-year-old's appearance. At that age they're still perfect." He grinned at me, reached over, and squeezed my hand. "I think you had a nightmare."

"But it isn't to improve his appearance, that's not her point at all. . . ." I swallowed, but I was in it now and there was no place to go but *on.* "She dyes her own, too."

"Well, I know, honey, and I wish she wouldn't, but that's so *different.* She's going gray early, and—"

"That's what she told me, too," I said. I got a sharp glance for that, and the temperature dropped in the car. I'd as good as called Kelsey a liar, and he was waiting for me to tell him why. "Daddy, she has to say that. She doesn't want us—or anybody—to know—something. A lot of things. Where she grew up. What she really looks like. I mean, it's a sort of *disguise.* The hair dye. For Preston too, maybe, because—"

"*Juni.* What in God's name . . . Dyed hair wouldn't disguise anybody—except maybe in that mystery yarn of yours! Kelsey grew up in eastern Washington. What's got into you?" Daddy sounded totally alarmed. But not about Kelsey or Preston's hair. About *me.*

Well, we never really got any further, though we talked at each other off and on for the next two hours—on, while we drank a milkshake at the Salem FrostyFridge; off, while he was concentrating on old Mr. Bainbridge's computer; on again, while we drove home. By that time I'd spilled the whole story—everything I'd been worrying about and snooping through Kelsey's things about and talking to Alison and Pete about. Well, nearly everything. I didn't tell him about tracking Blanche down—I didn't want another lecture about invasion of privacy.

Anyway, none of it did a bit of good. What it did was push a big fat block between me and Daddy. He saw no reason not to believe Kelsey's own accounts of her childhood, her first marriage, whatever. He didn't find it strange that all the labels had been taken out of her clothes. He sometimes cut *his* off, too—if they scratched his neck. In any case, he did *not*, repeat *not*, like my snooping through Kelsey's belongings. He was not at all thrilled to know I was discussing family matters—and fantasies—with my interested friends. I'm *glad* I didn't tell him about phoning Blanche.

By then he was sounding so stiff and—I don't know, *cold*—that I couldn't stand it, and couldn't keep the tears from coming up behind my eyes; and when that happens my eyes always get red and so does my *nose*, so I can't pretend I'm *not* crying, even though I *refuse* to really cry. I said, "My 'interested friends' are interested *because* they're my friends! They care about me! They—they—" My voice always shakes, too. "And anyway I'm not just making up *fantasies*."

"Juni. Honey. I think you are." The frost was gone from his voice, though. He suddenly slowed the car—we were on our way home—and I saw he was pulling off the freeway into one of the rest areas. His profile looked so—I don't know, so tired and worried—that all at once everything I'd been saying seemed as dumb to me as it probably did to him, and as unbelievable, and all I could feel was guilty. Especially when he stopped in the parking area and put his arms around me and just rubbed his beard against my hair awhile and let me cry.

"Juniper, baby," he said. "You're all shook up. You've just got yourself in a state, honey. I wish you'd told me before that you were worrying your head off about all this—this nothing. It's *nothing*. Just fantasy. Kelsey's true-blue all through, the way we used to say. . . ."

Margo used to say it. It only made me feel worse.

"Daddy, I don't think Kelsey's *bad*. Or not true-blue, or anything. I think she's *scared*. And hiding things. And she ought to tell us. Tell *you*. Because then you'd *help*."

"Of course I'd help. If she needed it. She'll tell me if and when she does."

I raised my head and looked straight at him and tried one more time. "Why don't you *ask* her, Daddy? Just ask her straight out what's the matter?"

"Honey bun, I don't think anything *is* the matter. If there is, I know she'll tell me, because we trust each other. Until she does, I'm not going to pry. There may be things she doesn't want to share with me, with anybody. That's her affair. People need a little emotional space to call their own."

And that was it.

I did say, "Will you let me show you, when we get home? Will you hold Preston still and *look* at his hair?"

"Of course, if it'll make you feel better," he answered.

Well, he did it. But the first thing I noticed when Preston ran over to hug me—he always does that now—was that his left eye was all red-looking. I said, "What's wrong, has he been crying?" and Kelsey said, "No, he's fine—I just got a little soap in his eye when I washed his hair."

Washed his hair. While we were gone. So of course when

Daddy kept his word, and looked, there was nothing to see. Dark brown clear to the scalp.

I suppose there never was any rusty-gold line. It was the sun or something, and I *have* just got myself into a state. It wouldn't be the first time. And Pete and Alison right along with me. We've probably been making up—*fantasies*—all summer. I feel stupid now, telling all that stuff to Daddy, and crying, and acting so dumb. He probably thinks I'm just jealous of Kelsey. I probably am.

Well, maybe now I *have* dumped the whole thing onto him, I'll be rid of it. It's not going to worry *him*, that's for sure.

10

My hair's all bleached streaky, the way it gets in summer. Daddy's is, too. In summer we're blond. In winter, mouse.

I'm going down to the pool for a while, later, with Pete and Alison. Unless I decide to stay home.

This morning Preston and I—

Oh, this is dumb. I can't write in this book anymore. It doesn't help. It doesn't help a bit.

Nothing else helps either, so I'm going to try again.

Alison leaves day after tomorrow to go to Minneapolis. I went over there this morning to help her decide what to pack. We laid everything out on her bed, in piles, real neat. She'll change her mind about most of them, she always does, and end by just grabbing whatever comes handy and stuffing it into her suitcase.

Maybe it's just as well she's leaving. I can't talk about Kelsey and all that anymore, I just can't. To her or Pete, either one.

It's all got too serious and miserable. But they don't know that, so they ask me how things are, and all I can do is pretend nothing new has happened, or try to laugh it off, the way I did at the pool yesterday, and just say I'm tired of that game. They didn't believe me, just looked at me kind of funny and dropped the subject. I guess I'm not a good actress, any more than Kelsey. Well, I know I'm not.

THURSDAY, AUGUST 8

Alison's gone. I went along when her mom took her to the airport, first thing this morning. We promised to write each other. She acted like she wanted to say a lot more—or wanted *me* to say something, but how could I? Without blabbing out *everything*, the baby and Preston's hair and feeling all wrong and far away from Daddy, and I'm not supposed to talk about some of that and anyway I can't. So I just had to shut Alison out the way Kelsey shuts me out, and I *hate* that.

She left me all her Elizabeth Kenilworth books to read— or reread—while she's away. I took them, because I didn't want to hurt her feelings, but I don't think I want to read any mysteries. Maybe not ever again. I guess I'll walk down to the library this afternoon, though. I have to read *something*, since I can't talk to anybody. Or have any fun or enjoy anything, because I'm just not in the mood. I suppose I could get ahead on some outside reading for social studies or something. Maybe I'll get some kind of big, thick biography of somebody dull. I might as well. Whatever I get I won't like it.

Wouldn't you know. I ran right into Pete on the library steps. He had a couple of books and was just leaving, so I said, "Oh. Hi," and kept right on going toward the doors, only that seemed so rude, and *mean*, because he'd stopped dead and was looking all sorts of questions at me; so I sort of hesitated and then turned back around.

He said, "You don't have to talk about anything you don't want to. But I'm sorry if it's something I did. Or said."

"No. Of course it isn't," I told him; then I ruined it by adding, "I mean, there isn't anything. What makes you think—"

"Don't bother," he said patiently. "But don't go off and be a hermit. There's about a million other things we can yak about. Why don't we walk over to the park and try some of them?"

I said okay, not really knowing whether it was a good idea or not, and came back down the steps to where he was, and stopped, sort of not looking anywhere in particular. I guess he could tell I was undecided. I guess anybody could have told, from a mile away. He didn't try to rush me, just waited.

"Were you going to get some books?" he asked me. "I don't mind hanging around."

"Oh—no—it doesn't matter. I mean, I was going to maybe get a head start on social studies. A biography of George Washington or something."

He just looked at me a minute. No comment. But I could feel myself beginning to grin, because I could hear how sorry for myself I sounded. As if I was homeless, and cross-eyed, and broke. I mean, hunting up a biography of George Washington *on purpose*, in *vacation time*, is about like saying you're going out in the garden and eat worms. I said, "Now I think of it, I'd rather walk over to the park."

He just said, "I should hope so," and we went on down the steps and across the street. We did walk to the park, and talked about things like teachers in eighth grade and a weirdo caterpillar with bright red fur that we found on the sidewalk, and all the new trees that were going to sprout up in the grass from those little propeller things that fall from the maples this time of year. We sat down on the little kids' swings for a while until some little kids came and stared at us; then we went over to Hill Road for frozen yogurt, and finally went home. And I feel lots better, more *comfortable* somehow, though we never said a word about the stuff that's bothering me.

Well, we nearly did once. I said, "Do you ever get at outs with your dad? I mean, feel like he isn't *listening?*"

"All the time," Pete said.

Well, that sounded sort of awful. I looked at him, really worried for a minute, but he smiled and said, "Not *all* the time," so I guess he just meant *It's normal. So what else is new?* I don't know why that should make me feel a little bit better, but it does.

It doesn't keep me from thinking, though. If you can call what I'm doing *thinking*. I just keep going over and over that half-minute on the escalator, first with Blanche staring, *certain* she had seen her nephew, then calmly on her way to the top, certain that she hadn't. *Why?* What in the world could have changed in those few seconds?

I'd better quit this and go to bed.

I think I know what happened in that few seconds on the escalator. I woke up, remembering.

I'm going to phone Blanche again, no matter how mad she gets.

Later

Not home. After all my artistic excuses to get out of the house and up to the 7-Eleven to use their phone. I *wish* Alison was still around so I could use hers. Well, I'll just have to do the whole thing again this afternoon.

Later

Still no luck!!!! I tried twice, with more than a half-hour in between. Even when I do get her, she'll probably take my head off for invading her privacy. I don't care.

Evening

After dinner I sort of hinted and offered to baby-sit, and Daddy and Kelsey took me up on it and went down to the Arts Cinema to some antique movie. All for nothing. I dialed Blanche four more times, then it got so late I didn't dare. Oh, *please* don't let her be out of town for the whole weekend!

SUNDAY, AUGUST 11

Something awful's happened. Kelsey's started campaigning to *move*. Out of our *house*. Clear out in the *boonies* somewhere.

I know she never meant for me to get wind of it so soon. But I slept kind of late this morning, so I made a piece of toast and just started eating it in my hand while I went to see where everybody was. Well, they were out back of the living room on that little terrace Daddy built when we got the barbecue, sitting in yard chairs and drinking coffee and watching Preston drag his little pull-toy duck around in the grass. I was about to slide open the screen door and go out too, but then I heard Kelsey saying, "It's Margo's house, really. I don't mean I dislike it, Charley. I *like* how colorful it is and everything. It's just that it's so much *her*, and I—well, I can't help but—"

Daddy said, real warm and supportive, "Of course you can't! Listen, sweet, it's my fault. I should've said, right at the beginning, 'Do the place over, new curtains, new paint'—"

"Oh—but so expensive! I've been thinking—how would you feel about ..." Kelsey hesitated, and I could see her swallow. I was standing there, frozen, on the other side of the screen door, thinking *But I don't* want *Margo's house changed, I don't* want *new curtains and new paint and everything different*; then she went on, real fast. "I just wondered how you'd feel about a different location. Maybe quite a ways out—away from traffic, and noise and all—like even the—the country. Not a farm, of course. Maybe an acre? We could have fruit trees, and room for a vegetable garden—"

I couldn't believe I was hearing straight. Traffic? Us and the neighbors, mooching up and down our little dead-end block to work and school and the store. Noise? In summer, lawn mowers and the Woodson boys dribbling a basketball out by their garage and once in a while a skateboard rattling down the slope. In winter, the blue jays are the noisiest things around. And we *do* have fruit trees—our Gravenstein apple and that wild yellow plum down in the woods beyond our yard, both about to get ripe about now, in case she hadn't noticed.

Well, she went on. About how handy it was that Daddy's office was in his hat and he could work from anywhere. About how great it would be for Preston to live in the country. He could have pets. A real duck. Maybe Juni could have a horse! The country was great for kids.

What kids? Preston, maybe. But what about *me?* I didn't *want* a horse. What about my *school,* and all the kids I grew up with, and *Alison,* and Pete, and everybody?

I know I should've let them know I was there. I knew I wasn't supposed to be in on this. But I just stood there, with my toast leaking jam into my hand, breathing hard, and feeling more and more helpless and frantic.

Daddy was looking down at his coffee cup, with that tired, worried, I-wish-this-wasn't-happening expression, and I knew he wanted to move about as bad as he wanted pellagra, but didn't know how to say so. I knew he *wouldn't* say no. He never has been the type to just put his big foot down and say *We're gonna do it my way.* He figures he's just one person in the family and he's got one vote.

And sure enough, he was nodding and trying to smile at her, and saying, "We'll have to think."

Before I knew I was going to, I shoved the screen open so hard it banged, and was out there with them, crying, "*Why* do we have to think? *I* don't have to think! I vote *no,* N, O! I don't *want* to move! Why should I have to leave my friends, and my school, and—"

"Juni! Cool it!" Daddy was on his feet, Kelsey wide-eyed, both of them staring at me as if I'd sprung from the moon. Daddy started toward me. "Honey child. We didn't know you were anywhere around."

"Well, it's a good thing I was! First thing I knew I'd have been yanked out of my own school—and right in the middle, too, in eighth grade!—and put into some country school with a lot of new kids I don't even *know*—and then I'd have to go to some other *high school*, have you thought of that? Well, I won't, I can't! I want to go to *Hillridge High* like I've always planned, because it just happens to be one of the best high schools in the Portland *area*, and. . . ." And so on.

Naturally, I shouldn't have said a word of it, I should've let it choke me first. Because catch anybody paying attention to *my* vote, especially with my voice shaking and the decibels turned all the way up.

Daddy finally said, "That'll do, Juniper!" in the voice that says *I mean it*. Then he went on, quietly, but as if he had his teeth gritted, "This was a private—and very *preliminary*—conversation. Nothing at all is settled about moving. It wouldn't be the end of the world if it were."

"It would," I said. By that time I *was* kind of choking. "It'd be the end of *my* world."

"No, it wouldn't, whether you think so or not. And other people's needs have to be considered. That's all we're doing, considering. I realize you can't be expected to understand, but it's hard for Kelsey. . . . It's hard for any woman to live in another woman's house. She—"

"That's not it!" I cried. "That's not the reason she wants to move at all! *Is* it, Kelsey?"

"*Juniper Webb!*" Daddy snapped out.

Well, I shut up. I knew I'd blown it. Kelsey was looking as if I'd just hit her in the face, and Daddy hadn't missed it. And anyway, wouldn't you *know*, I'd got such a death grip on my toast that now I had a handful of mush and jelly I didn't know what to do with, and how can you make anybody think of you as a real person, with real arguments, and a *vote*, when you've got mixed up in a third-rate comedy routine?

I said, "I'm *sorry!*" and ran—back through the living room to the kitchen to get rid of that *stupid* toast, and then went up the stairs three at a time and locked myself in my room.

Crying didn't help much, though it got me past wanting to yell and kick and hate somebody, and left me just feeling hopeless and tireder than I ever remember feeling. By the time Daddy spoke to me through my door about half an hour later, I was ready to let him in.

Of course, that didn't help either. He was calm but stern, and said all the things I expected. That Kelsey was under a lot of stress and couldn't take much more. That he realized she was oversensitive, overprotective of Preston, inclined to be nervous. I must remember she's pregnant. She so much wanted to be friends and she'd tried and I'd been making it very difficult. And he thought I owed her an apology for that remark I'd flung at her—whatever it was supposed to mean.

"I'm sorry I said that," I told him—and I *am*, because all it did was make him mad and put me in the wrong. I did try to convince him that *I* think Kelsey's running away from some sort of danger—but I guess it just sounded like I was making an excuse. He said the only danger for Kelsey was a nervous breakdown if I didn't try to avoid upsetting her.

It was no use trying to explain everything—in fact, anything. Even if I'd known how. I guess it's no wonder he thinks I'm just inventing stuff. There's a lot he doesn't know a thing about. And so much I'm not really sure of that I sometimes wonder, myself, if I'm just making it up. So I just nodded, and he put his arm around me and rubbed his beard against my hair, and left.

114

Writing in this book has helped a little—kind of calmed me down. Maybe I'll never be able to explain all that about Kelsey. But I've got to explain to him how I feel about moving. Maybe this evening, before he's had a chance to think too hard about Kelsey's needs and everything. I've got to talk to him calmly and *reasonably*. I mean, I have lots of *good* reasons and a right to my vote. Haven't I? He's not always going to do every single thing Kelsey wants him to, forever—is he? I still count too, don't I?

Later

I decided to try Blanche one more time before I talked to Daddy. About four o'clock I walked up to 7-Eleven and dialed the number. By now I know it by heart.

She was there. I got stage fright and nearly dropped the phone but I somehow gabbled out, "Ms. Mitchell, this is Marianne again, but *please* don't hang up till I ask you just one question because it's *really* important and not just a bet with my friend." I didn't give her a chance to say no, just barged right on and asked her *why* she was sure, and *when* she was sure that little boy wasn't her nephew.

Well, she barely hung on to her patience, but she told me. "I was sure when he took off his hat. My nephew has red hair."

I *knew* it.

I didn't even hear her bawling me out, if she did, or telling me not to phone again, I was so busy thinking of that one-eighth-inch of rusty-gold at Preston's hairline, and *seeing* him, there on the escalator, pulling off his hat to uncover a head of dark brown hair.

Daddy can say "dyed hair is no disguise" if he wants to. This time it was—and it worked. That's what *I* think. But he doesn't listen to what I think. I had to *know*.

I said, "Did . . . his mother . . . ever call him 'Bitsy'?"

There was a dead silence at the other end of the phone. Then suddenly she asked, sounding breathless, as if I'd hit her in the solar plexus, "What do you know about his mother?" I didn't say anything and she went on, her voice harsh and urgent. "Where is the boy? Who are you, anyway? Marianne—? Marianne! What did you say your last name was? Marianne, are you still there?"

I said, "Yes," but I had to gulp for breath, too.

"Then answer me! Where is he? How do you know about him?"

I sort of whispered, "I can't tell you. I can't tell you anything else."

"Of course you can! You've got to. Tell me where you live—the address. Your phone number. I've got to talk to you. . . ."

The demanding voice went on squawking out of the phone but all I could hear was Pete saying *You'd better find out* all *about this before you go blowing the whistle.* . . . Finally Blanche's voice stopped. The dial tone was buzzing in my ear before I remembered to hang up.

So now I'm certain. I'm not making things up. Something is really, really wrong. Because Kelsey's *still* trying to run away. In fact she wants us *all* to run away now from our own perfectly good house and hide in the country.

Maybe it's time to blow the whistle. I've got to do something. Daddy's got to listen.

11

I know I can't put it off any longer. I've got to get it all down, so it'll be straight in my mind when I write Alison—when I can bear to—and as Pete said yesterday, so I'll remember facts and plain truth instead of just my *feelings* about everything. Actually, I don't think I'll ever forget a single fact *or* feeling about the last three days if I live to be a hundred and fifty.

I don't know how to start.

Well—I blew the whistle on Kelsey. Last Sunday evening about an hour or so after I wrote in this book, I got Daddy to listen. I did it by dropping a bomb. And ever since, I've felt like somebody who's dropped a real bomb because pieces flew everywhere and innocent people are probably going to get hurt—*Preston*, for one, *especially* little Preston—all because of me.

Okay, okay. Facts, not feelings.

At the time, I was *full* of feelings, just desperate to do something, anything, because I didn't want to move to the country, because Daddy wouldn't pay attention. I waited till Preston was in bed and the rest of us were in the kitchen stacking the dishwasher. Then I asked Kelsey straight out if she knew anybody named Blanche Mitchell.

117

She let go of the plate she was holding. It hit the edge of the counter, cracked against the open dishwasher door, and smashed into fragments on Margo's Mexican-tile floor.

For a minute we all froze, like a video on pause—Kelsey clinging to the counter as if she couldn't stand upright, Daddy with a platter in his hand, staring at her, me beginning to turn numb and scared, while a final little shard of our blue-rimmed everyday china spun around on its bottom and finally settled. I knew already I should never have opened my mouth.

Then Daddy quickly put aside the platter and bent over Kelsey, pulling her up against him and saying angrily, "Juni, what are you talking about?"

All I could say was, "Ask *her. Please.*"

He glared and said, "I'm asking *you*," but Kelsey shook her head and made vague motions with her hand, and he went back to peering at her, holding her by the shoulders and frowning into her face. She was white and thin-looking, her freckles plain, and the bones of her face sharp, and her eyes darker than usual and sort of unfocused. He said, "You're going to sit down. Then we're going to talk about this. Juni, get her some water."

I did that, fast, and he made her drink a little, then walked her to the breakfast nook and put her in one chair and sat down in the next one, and gave a jerk of his head at me. So I went over there, too—not feeling my feet—and slid into a chair across from them.

Kelsey didn't say a word, just sat there with her shoulders slumped, looking exhausted. And Daddy finally did what I'd been begging him to do. He took hold of her, gently, and turned her to face him, and said, "Kelsey, baby. What's wrong? Whatever it is, I'm with you. All the way. Come on, get it off your chest. Juni insists you're in some kind of trouble. 'Dan-

118

ger,' she says." He halfway smiled at the word, even then. "Are you? Tell me."

For a minute she just looked at him, with this terribly *sad* expression—as if she was trying to memorize his face, as if she might never get to look at it again. Then she took a long, tired-sounding breath and said, "Not me. Or maybe I am, but that doesn't matter. It's Preston."

I got this sudden knot in my throat even though I *knew* she was going to say that—at least, I'd dreaded it, all along. Daddy just looked baffled, then almost relieved.

"*Preston?*" he said. "Well, you can quit worrying right now. I'll protect Preston! Why, I'd defend him with my life—you *know* that, Kelsey! If for no reason but that he's *your* little boy."

She smiled at him, painfully, but almost as if *he* was the little boy. "Charley . . ." she said. She hesitated one last time, then came out with it. "He's not my little boy. He's my little brother."

Her little brother.

There it was—the key to everything—finally out in the open and staring us in the face, while Daddy and I stared back.

All the puzzle pieces in my mind were spinning in a kind of whirlwind and gradually settling down into a brand-new pattern. Her little *brother*. It began to make a sort of sense.

I guess it didn't to Daddy. He said, "*Step*brother?"

"No, no, Charley. My own brother, Robert Shelby. My mother's child. That's the trouble," Kelsey added desperately. "He's not mine."

"But—" Daddy was still struggling with the bare idea. "You've got a brother *twenty-three* years younger than you?"

Kelsey took another long breath and swallowed hard. "I lied about my age, Charley. I—I'm just nineteen."

"Nine*teen?*" said Daddy, sounding stunned.

I was pretty startled, too, though I've always thought Kelsey looked younger than twenty-five—lots younger. Well, heavens, she's only six years older than *me*. Or anyway that's what it'll be when I'm thirteen, two weeks from now. No wonder I could never think of her as a mother. Nineteen—that's like a *big sister*. Which is something I never dreamed I'd have.

"God help me," Daddy said in this unreal voice. "And I already thought I was—was robbing the cradle."

"Oh, Charley, I'm *sorry*," said Kelsey. She clasped both hands together, tight, and hid her face for a minute, then straightened up and added, "I might've known I'd spoil it somehow. I did know, really."

"Now, take it easy," Daddy told her. I thought he looked as if he was finding it hard to take it easy himself, as if he was saying "nineteen" over and over in his head. But he said, "Just relax and tell me. Your mother is dead?"

"Dead drunk, more likely," said Kelsey, in that same flat, hard voice, like when she'd talked about drug users that time. Her expression matched the voice. She suddenly seemed older, though she'd just told us she was younger. She seemed almost like somebody else.

Well, she *is* somebody else—just as I always suspected. She's Sharonlee Shelby from Boise, Idaho, as she told us right then, though I'll never, never think of her that way. But before this I hadn't *seen* the person she was trying to change from, trying to escape. Neither had Daddy. He settled back slowly in his chair, watching her, looking as if he was bracing himself against he didn't know what. He said, "Go on."

"Well, you can guess, can't you?" Kelsey burst out. "I stole Bitsy from her. I just—left her. To go ahead and drink herself to death. My own mother. I—I didn't know what else to do."

Daddy said gently, "Start at the beginning."

Instead, Kelsey said, "Juniper, how much did you tell Aunt Blanche? You must have talked to her." She studied her hands when she said it—as if she couldn't bear the sight of me. I couldn't blame her.

"Nothing," I said. "I guess she's—pretty sure Preston is her nephew, Robert." It seemed funny to call him that. "Bitsy" suited him lots better. But all at once I realized why Kelsey had panicked the day I'd heard her say it. Even his real *nickname* had to be kept secret in case someone recognized it—and, in fact, Aunt Blanche had.

"You must have told her *something*," Kelsey said.

"Not really. She knows he's Robert but she doesn't know our name for him, or my name, or where we live. She thinks I'm somebody called Marianne."

Daddy turned to stare at me. "Is it catching?" he demanded.

For a second I just stared back at him, with my mouth ajar, then I saw what he meant. Everybody but him was now going by an alias. Sharonlee was Kelsey. Robert-Bitsy was Preston. And I was Marianne. Marianne Jackson, from Northeast Stark. I mumbled, "Well, it was the first name I thought of. I didn't want to give away anything that might—"

"She'll find us. Sooner or later," Kelsey said. "I don't know why I thought I could get away with it. It was stupid. And now it's over. Everything's over." She took off her wedding ring and laid it on the table in front of Daddy. "You won't want to stay married to me when you find out what all I've done—how I've lied and pretended—" Daddy grabbed the ring, jammed it back on her finger and held her hand, tight. "But Charley, I *stole* Preston," she burst out, as if she thought Daddy hadn't heard. "I just—ran off with him. I knew it was wrong but I had to. You don't know how it was—I'd come home after school and find him wet, and miserable, and crying kind of *hopelessly*, as if he'd been at it for hours—hungry, too, and she'd be—out like a light, there in the back bedroom. . . . I couldn't . . . I *couldn't* be there all the time. I had to work after school and Saturdays, because she'd lost the shop, and there wasn't much money left, and—"

"You were working *and* going to high school? Where was your father? Where is he now?"

"I don't know. He took off again—months before Bitsy was born. He doesn't even know he's got another kid. He figured I was old enough to get away on my own, this time. He told me to finish high school and get out, that he wasn't coming back. He left me some money. Three hundred dollars. It wasn't enough to go far, but—"

"Why in God's name didn't he take you *with* him?" demanded Daddy.

"He tried to, one time. When I was about five years old. That's when he left before. He got fed up because Mom— well, she was in one of her real bad times. He was going to get custody of me and just leave her to it. They wouldn't let him have me."

"Who wouldn't?"

"The—you know. Authorities. A judge. You don't know my mom. She can snap herself out of it and fool anybody— social workers—anybody. Even her partner in the shop—over and over. Even Aunt Blanche sometimes. They all think *this* time it's going to work, she's going to stay sober, and a child ought to be with its mother. Well, she never sticks it out. She never has, in all my life."

"All your life," Daddy said softly—only to himself, I think, but Kelsey answered him.

"All I can remember. But there used to be good spells—a couple of months, maybe a whole summer. Now she can't even get through a day. I think she's on drugs, too." Kelsey took a long breath. "After Bitsy was born it got worse. It was as if she blamed *him* for being there, on her hands—in her way. I came home one day and she was *shaking* him. Hard. You can injure a baby's brain that way! Charley, I *had* to take him. I *had* to get him out of there."

"Yes," Daddy said quietly. "Of course you did. Maybe not exactly—the *way* you did. If you'd reported all this to Children's Services—"

"They'd have put him in a foster home! Given him to strangers!"

"Honey—I think they would've let you take him."

"They wouldn't, they wouldn't!" Kelsey's voice had gone shrill, and I could see tears flashing in her eyes. "Give him to a teenager just out of high school? No chance! They wouldn't even let my own father take *me* that time, and he was a grown man, with a job! I was *losing* my job—the shop was sold—"

"All right. I see. I see." Daddy dragged her chair closer to his and pulled her into his arms. "Go back a little. Tell me about this shop."

It took him an hour, but he gradually coaxed it all out of her. I didn't say a word. I mean, I've already butted in too much. But we finally got the story pretty straight. Her mother—Ruth Shelby—used to be partners with a woman named Marie Morgan in this beauty shop in Boise, Idaho, when Kelsey was growing up. Blanche worked there, too, which I guess was a good thing, because she used to cover for Kelsey's mom when she'd show up drunk, or not show up at all.

"But then after work Aunt Blanche would come out to our house and bawl Mom out and swear this was the last time—and that only made Mom yell at her, and scared me, especially when I was little, because I thought they were mad at *me*. I used to climb up in the attic and hide until my dad came home. I hate loud voices, I still go into a kind of cold sweat when people yell at each other."

People like me, I thought guiltily. Nobody else except Preston ever raises a voice around here.

"Did your dad do anything about it when he did show up?" Daddy asked her. I think he was madder at her father than at her mother, who in my opinion was causing all the trouble.

"I don't know," Kelsey said wearily. "Maybe he tried. He always came up to the attic and got me, and took me down to bed. But nothing ever changed. The trouble was, my dad was always gone a lot. I mean, gone from Boise."

"What's his work?"

"I don't know what it is now. In those days he mostly drove for a big moving company, so he'd be clear across the country about half the time. Sometimes he worked for truckers around Idaho. Once he traveled with a carnival for a while—ran the Ferris wheel. I guess he's a sort of restless type." Kelsey glanced up at Daddy with an apologetic little half-smile, then looked away again and shrugged. "Anyway, what could he do? He couldn't make Mom stop drinking. Nobody could."

Daddy didn't say anything, and I couldn't have if I'd tried. It must have been awful to have a mother like that, and grow up like that, with nobody taking care of you, and your father never around when you needed him. When I think of Daddy— and Margo . . .

Well, anyway, last winter this Marie Morgan decided she wanted to retire, and move with her daughter and son-in-law to—guess where—Australia (just like Kelsey's made-up brother). The son-in-law was going to help run his father's sheep ranch. Marie Morgan had already bought Ruth Shelby out of the business, a couple of years back—well, anybody could see she *had* to. So now she sold the whole shop to this chain called Mr. Pierre. They brought in their own hair stylists and gave most of the old employees notice. Blanche, for one, and Kelsey. Blanche left pretty soon—she had an offer from a Seattle wholesaler who used to supply the shop. All Kelsey had was that three hundred dollars. And Preston to rescue.

She said, "I knew I had to get him away, while I still had that money. But I didn't know where to go so nobody'd find us. Or how to stay hidden. I might never have figured it out if I hadn't—hadn't—" She swallowed. "Hadn't remembered Kay's purse."

Kay? This was a brand-new character we'd never heard of— much less her purse. Kelsey had stopped talking.

Daddy said, "Honey? Who is Kay?"

For a minute I thought she wasn't going to tell us. It seemed harder for her than all the rest. She had to swallow again and moisten her lips. Then finally she said, "Marie Morgan's daughter—Kelsey. Her nickname's Kay."

Daddy and I both sat there blinking at her—I was busy adding two and two and two, and so must Daddy have been, because pretty soon he said, "Kelsey Morgan. The daughter who had moved to Australia."

"Yes."

"With her husband—Tim Blockman?"

"Jim," Kelsey said.

That figured. It explained her slip that time.

Daddy said, "You found a purse of hers—with her ID in it?"

"She'd *given* me the purse. She was always giving me clothes and things that she'd outgrown or was through with—all my life. Hand-me-downs, they were, but I never minded. She was my *friend*. Like an older sister or cousin or something. You don't know how I hated to see her go." Kelsey's voice shook a little, but pretty soon she went on. "Well—she'd given me this old summer purse along with some other things, just before she left. It was awhile before I even looked inside it. Then I noticed the lining had pulled loose, and something had slipped inside there. I fished it out—it was one of those little plastic folders, with Kay's driver's license and Social Security card and voter registration card in it. I remember she had to replace all that stuff, along in the fall—she thought she'd lost it. Of course by the time I found it she was long gone. I meant to send it to her, but I never did. Then later I—I remembered about it."

Daddy was nodding—I expect I was, too. It was all getting pretty clear. She'd looked at that ID and simply decided to turn into Kelsey Morgan Blockman and vanish to Portland with a suddenly acquired small son.

"Why Portland?" Daddy asked her.

Kelsey shrugged. "It was the closest big town. Big enough, I *thought*, so I'd never run into anybody I ever knew. I thought Aunt Blanche was in Seattle! Besides, as soon as we got here I dyed my hair and Bitsy's too—just in case."

It had worked too. Or would have, except for me and my meddling.

She'd had to do it. She and Preston both have red hair under the dye—his sort of rusty-gold, like that little trace I saw, and hers more copper. They'd have been easy to spot, if anybody was looking. Besides, Kay's hair was dark, and Kelsey had to match the description and picture on that driver's license. She'd already destroyed the precinct card from Kay's wallet and whatever labels there were in her own clothes; she took only dresses and skirts and things that made her look older, because

126

Kay was twenty-five. She even left her favorite blue sweater behind, because Kay never wore that color. She thought of *everything*. Once the dye jobs were done she made up her face and did her hair to look as much like Kay's picture as she could, and practiced Kay's signature. Then she applied for an Oregon driver's license.

"It took me a whole morning to get myself out of that motel and into the nearest DMV office. I knew I had to do it. To get my own picture on a new license. But I was so *scared*." Kelsey closed her eyes, just thinking about it.

"They didn't question you?" asked Daddy.

She shook her head. "It was a dumb picture of Kay—it could've been anybody, almost. They barely looked at it anyway."

"So then?"

"So then I got a cheap room. And found a day-care center. And looked for a job. I didn't dare try for the kind of work I was used to. A beauty shop's the first place anybody'd look for me. But I can type—we had word processors in high school. I got taken on at Quickhelp. That kept us going—more or less. Then one of the places I went as a temporary hired me steady. It was that title company where you came that day to install their new system." Kelsey looked at Daddy. "And I met you."

For a long time, nobody said anything.

"And that's the end of the story," she finished quietly.

But it wasn't. It *isn't*. I know what Alison—or rather, Elizabeth Kenilworth—would say: It was the end of the *exposition*, the part we hadn't known before. It's the *middle* of the story, or maybe the crisis, because here we all are, with the situation as unstable as ever and nothing resolved at all. Preston is still stolen. Kelsey is still using somebody else's name and ID.

Ruth Shelby is still back in Boise, Idaho, drinking herself to death. Blanche is still trying to find her nephew. And Kelsey's carefully worked out rescue plan is ruined—thanks to meddling Juniper.

That's what I was thinking about.

Daddy wasn't. He said gently, "That's why you married me? To get a home for Preston?"

Kelsey's face sort of crumpled. She whispered, "Oh, *no*, Charley! No, no. I married you because I love you. *Please* believe me."

I believed her. It had been plain as daylight all along—you only had to see them together and watch her face. But Daddy was watching it now with a sort of sad, painful anxiety that made me have to look away. In fact, I decided they definitely didn't need some dumb twelve-year-old kid around right now, kibitzing. I sort of eased away and went upstairs. I don't think they missed me.

I *can't* have ruined their marriage, along with everything else. Daddy's *got* to see that to her he doesn't seem old, that he's more than just security, he's everything, a sort of perfect person. They'll work it out—I keep telling myself. But it's still not exactly—settled—even now, three whole days later. I can feel it sort of hanging in the air. I can tell Daddy's thinking *nineteen*, and feeling thirty-five going on thirty-six. Also he's probably replaying in his mind all his lecturing to me about "inventing fantasies" and "trusting each other," and remembering how firmly he believed it—*then*—and wondering if he can forget about Kelsey's lies.

Except that they hurt Daddy so bad, *I* can forget about them—because of Preston. I'm right behind every single thing Kelsey did, though I haven't dared tell her that yet—or say much of anything else to her. I figure the less she sees of me right now the better she'll like it. But every time I hug Preston, or hear him laughing, or try to put socks on his rubbery little feet, I'm *gladder* she did what she did, and I don't care what she had to do, to get him away. I'll bet this Kay wouldn't have minded a bit about her ID. I'll bet she'd have *helped* Kelsey pretend to be her. *I* would've.

I think Kelsey's the bravest person in the world. I could never have been that brave. Or that smart. I think she's just *wonderful*—and I might never have known that if I hadn't blown her cover. So in that way, it's a big relief to have the air cleared, and all the doubts and wrong guesses—the whole mystery mess—behind us. But I'll just *die* if she doesn't stay right here, and stay married to Daddy, so we can all be together.

The two of them are still a mile apart as to how that's going to happen. Daddy says the only way to be truly safe is to bring the whole thing out in the open, and settle it legally—put it into a lawyer's hands. Kelsey begs and pleads with him not to. She says they'll take Preston away.

But what if he does it anyhow? Will she have to give Preston back? Will they put her in jail? I don't *know*. And when I think about that, I don't see how she can ever forgive me for ruining everything. I don't see how Daddy can, either.

I don't even see how I can forgive myself.

12

Nothing is settled yet. Far from it.

I talked to Pete again this morning, sitting beside him on our favorite park bench, which has a lot of open grass around it so you know nobody can overhear—same place we talked on Monday, the day after I blew the lid off.

Maybe I shouldn't be telling him all this private, family stuff. But he knows so much of it anyway, and Alison's gone, and I *have* to talk to somebody. I'm being sort of—ignored—at home. I mean, Daddy and Kelsey are mostly worrying about each other, and about Preston. Daddy has to go out on his jobs every day, and Kelsey mooches around the house with the walk-around phone in her pocket so she can take his clients' calls, and they both look like they're sleepwalking. I'm trying to be useful though invisible until they make up their minds how they feel about me. I mean, they probably can't decide whether I've done us all a favor, or just opened Pandora's box; and whichever it is they don't have time to think about it yet.

I don't blame them a bit. "I can't even decide that, myself," I told Pete. "Because how do I know what's going to happen now?"

"What do you think's going to happen?" Pete asked.

"I think Daddy's going to talk to Mr. Adams—that's his lawyer—when Mr. Adams gets back from vacation Monday. He *says* he's going to. And when he says something in that tone of voice, kind of quiet and even, it means he *will*."

"And Kelsey's still against it."

"Dead set. She's terrified of dragging it all out in the open, to be decided by a judge. Judges give children back to their mothers—that's all she can think of. Daddy says it'll be different, now she's married and has a stable home. But if their marriage is going to be kind of rocky . . ."

"You think it is?"

"I don't know," I said miserably. I *felt* miserable. I still do. It isn't that Daddy doesn't understand everything Kelsey did—telling lies about her name and age and all. I mean, he realizes what she was up against. But I don't think he understands why she lied to *him*. He says, "Why didn't you tell me long ago?" And she says, "I *wanted* to. You don't know how much I wanted to! But I didn't dare, I couldn't let *anybody* know for fear it would get out, then they'd take Bitsy away. I couldn't let it happen. I *can't* let it happen. You don't know what it's like."

And he sort of nods, but after a while he asks her again, maybe in different words. The way he'd figure—if she really loves him and knows he really loves her, why couldn't she trust him with the truth? He absolutely trusted *her*, and believed everything she said. So now he probably sort of feels like a fool. I think that's what hurts him. It would me.

Daddy probably trusts all sorts of people he shouldn't be trusting. I suppose that *is* being a fool. But, oh, I'd hate for him to change.

I didn't say any of this to Pete, of course. I have *some* sense

131

of family privacy. All I said was, "If only I'd never butted in! The whole mess is all my fault."

"No, it is not," Pete said in this severe, teachery tone of voice. "It is all Kelsey's mother's fault. Don't go getting over-emotional and sorry for yourself. That won't do any good."

"Well, you don't need to bawl me out!" I snapped.

"Well, I think I did," he said reasonably.

He may have been right. I guess I was kind of wallowing around in my own guilt feelings. It made sense to quit that, at any rate. I said, "So tell me what *will* do any good, if you're so smart."

"We'll have to think," Pete told me patiently. "We've both got brains. We'll have to use 'em."

He didn't have any suggestions, though. "I wish Alison was here," I said. Then I sort of heard how that sounded, and apologized.

But all Pete said was, "I know what you mean."

So *he's* not much use to me so far. I wrote Alison day before yesterday and explained how things had turned out, and told her *strictly* never to say one word to *anyone, ever*, about our stupid mystery game. How I wish we'd never played it! How I wish Elizabeth Kenilworth had never come to our school at all! I'd have done better to spend that *entire period* on math.

I guess I'll go take Preston out for a buggy-ride. If it weren't for Preston, I'd feel like a sort of nonperson around this house. But *he* still likes me just the same.

MONDAY, AUGUST 19

Daddy's found a compromise. I guess. He phoned Mr. Adams today and made an appointment for Thursday, with Kelsey

132

right there hearing him do it, and biting her knuckles trying not to cry. I heard him, too. I didn't actually mean to, but I was just passing by on my way upstairs, and how could I help it? He wasn't trying to keep it private, the study door was wide open.

He didn't lower his voice, either, just said, "Honey, we've got to find out where we stand legally. I'm not going to betray you. I won't reveal a thing, I'll keep it theoretical. Ostensibly I'll be there on other business—to make small revisions in my clients' service contracts."

"He won't believe you," Kelsey all but whispered.

"He will. Trust me. You can, you know."

Ouch. Kelsey didn't answer. I don't blame her. I don't blame her for worrying, either. How do you keep a question like that theoretical? Say it's for a friend? Mr. Adams has known Daddy for years, knows about our family—he was at the wedding. Seems to me the "friend's" new family would strike him as a good bit like ours. But Pete told me yesterday that even if he suspects anything—or everything—it won't matter.

"Won't *matter?*" I said.

"Not a bit. He won't tell anybody *else*. It'll be privileged information. Lawyers are like doctors."

"How do you know so much about it?"

"I'm going to *be* one."

Yes, well. That doesn't prove anything about Daddy's plan. I only hope it works.

THURSDAY, AUGUST 22, EVENING

Maybe he's pulled it off. *He* thinks so, anyway. What Mr. Adams thinks is anybody's guess.

"Did you tell him it was for a friend?" I asked nervously. Believe me, I was as nervous as Kelsey.

"No." Daddy looked at me. "I told him my daughter was writing a mystery, and needed to know."

That shut my mouth, since I couldn't think of a single thing to say. Kelsey was surprised enough to be distracted for a moment. "*Are* you?" she asked.

"Well, I was," I mumbled.

"Adams never questioned it," Daddy told her. "And he gave me a considered and very encouraging answer." He smiled down into Kelsey's anxious face. "He said in his opinion no court in the land would give Preston back into his mother's custody—unless her situation is vastly changed—and no court would prosecute a sibling for stepping in."

I couldn't see that Kelsey was all that much relieved; she kept looking at him, chewing her lower lip, and obviously thinking hard. "That doesn't mean they'd give him to me, though."

"Adams seemed to think they would. Unless—"

Kelsey pounced on that. "Unless what?"

"Well—unless your mother's situation is vastly changed," Daddy repeated. Kelsey just waited. He shrugged and added, "Or unless some other family member should step in to oppose it. But that needn't worry—"

"I knew there'd be a joker," Kelsey said.

"But darling, there's no such person around. Your father's God knows where—"

"There's Aunt Blanche."

Daddy had forgotten about Aunt Blanche. Or discounted her, maybe. "But—wouldn't she be *glad* to see Preston properly cared for?"

"By a good foster family. Not by me!"

"I can't believe that."

"Charley, she wouldn't trust me to care for a kitten properly. If there's trouble to make, she'll make it." She went on, sounding desperate. Blanche had opposed her dad taking *her* that time—and he'd lost his case. She can't *talk* to Blanche. Blanche stonewalls her. Blanche won't *listen*. Not to her. "To her I'm just an 'overemotional teenager.' And I'm 'just like my father'—she's said that all my life, and what she means is unstable, unreliable, un-everything. I'm just a—a *nothing*." Kelsey practically spat it out.

It seemed to be a stalemate. Daddy said finally, "There's only one way to be certain how she'll react—contact her and find out."

Well, Kelsey panicked. I guess she's always felt intimidated by Blanche—and I know just why. "Charley, I can't! I won't! You don't know her—she'll just say I've proved it by doing this crazy thing I did—"

"But the court will see it as 'stepping in,'" Daddy said patiently. "Kelsey, we can't let Preston grow up thinking you're his mother. He's bound to find out different. Then *he'll* have a problem."

"No, I—I'll explain. I'll make him understand. . . ."

It went on for quite a while. And ended when Daddy said, "You needn't have anything to do with it. *I'll* talk to your Aunt Blanche. What's the name of that firm she works for?"

Kelsey was quiet a minute and then said, "Charley, I won't tell you."

After another minute that seemed to go on and on, and we all knew what was coming, Daddy turned and looked at me.

Because of course, *I* know. The name of the firm. Even Blanche's home phone number. And the truth is, I'm on Daddy's side. We've just got to get Preston for keeps, and the only way to do it is legally.

But he needn't think I'm going to rat on Kelsey. Not again. I just shook my head, and ran upstairs, and locked my door.

SATURDAY, AUGUST 24

Alison phoned me this evening. Oh, it was *great* to talk to her! And for a wonder Daddy had taken Kelsey to a movie—"to get her mind off it all" he said—and I'd already put Preston to bed so there was nothing to keep Alison and me from yakking as long and hard as we wanted. Except the phone bill, of course. But her dad had told her thirty minutes was the limit, and we managed to stop in only forty-five.

She'd got my letter, and I caught her up with the rest of what's happened, and then answered questions about Pete, and she told me a lot of stuff about concerts and the new school outfit her dad's bought her, and then we kind of ran down and just sat for a minute listening to the miles between us faintly humming over all those far-off wires.

Then she said, "The trouble is, he knows her last name, doesn't he?"

I didn't need to ask who she was talking about. "I guess so. He heard me say it—only once, though, that Sunday when I blew the whistle. He might have forgotten it."

"If he hasn't, he could track her down in the phone book same as we did."

"I don't think he's tried. I think he wants Kelsey to change her mind."

"He'll get tired of that."

"Yes, well, power to him, then. But it won't be *my* fault."

Alison was silent a minute—analyzing my character, I could tell. "You want him to find Blanche," she decided.

"I guess so. I don't *know*. He'd probably spill everything in the first five minutes—what our name is and where we live and *everything*. He's so *honest*. Then what if she decided to make trouble? There'd be nothing to stop her."

"So you *don't* want him to find her, or her to find you—you just want to know what she'd do?"

"Yeah," I said.

There was another little silence, while our great minds ran in the same channel. "So?" said Alison. "You better ask her."

I didn't bother to explode with *Me? What are you talking about? Why me? I can't phone her again, she'd kill me!*—though it was all on the tip of my tongue. Alison would just argue me down with the same arguments I've been hearing inside my head the whole past couple of days. *I* knew how to get hold of Blanche. *I* wouldn't give anything away. She couldn't *really* kill me over the phone. I said, "You always have such great ideas. For *me*."

I could practically hear Alison shrug. "Just don't tell her anything. Say you have to know how she feels about it. She'll come around. Lemme know how it turns out," she added.

She's so sure I'm going to do it—stick my head right in the lion's mouth. Well, *I'm* not sure. Not yet.

SUNDAY, AUGUST 25

I can't stand it any longer. The tension around this house has even percolated down to Preston—he's been as cranky as a soaking-wet bee the whole morning. It's no way to live. I'd rather be struck dead over the phone.

So I walked up to the 7-Eleven half an hour ago and dialed Blanche's number and prayed she wouldn't be home. But of course she was. I said, "This is Marianne."

There was a brief silence, which sounded to me like a grim setting of her jaw. "*Well,* Marianne," she said in exactly the sort of voice I expected. "I've been hoping you'd call. To finish what you started. To answer my questions."

"Yes. I—if I can."

"You *must* answer them. You *must,* do you hear me? Where is my nephew? How do you know about him? What do you know about his mother?"

"I know all about everything," I said, hoping I really did know all of it now, that there weren't any little bits and pieces Kelsey hadn't bothered to mention—or was scared to mention. "Sh-Sharonlee told me."

Another tiny pause. "I see," Blanche said. Her voice had gone all sort of stiff and wooden. As if she hated it that I knew all about her sister. Well, I didn't blame her. After a minute she said, "Sharonlee's here, then. In Portland. What has she done with Robert?"

"He's perfectly safe."

"I'll be the judge of that! Tell me where he *is.*"

"Ms. Mitchell—I want to. But I can't. Yet. I was thinking maybe we ought to—talk."

"I've been thinking *you* ought to. The sooner the better."

"I mean—like—in person. Maybe today." I figured it was talking on the phone that bugged me. I like to *see* people when I say things to them. Not just guess how they feel.

"All right. Where?" Blanche said.

"Well—I thought—the mall?"

138

"Where in the mall?"

My mind scrambled wildly around the mall, searching for privacy. "Maybe Grover Brothers' fourth floor? The offices'll be closed on Sunday, and there's a bench—"

"Yes. Now you be there. Two o'clock."

"Okay."

I expected her to say "And be on *time*," but she only hung up. So I did, too, and pushed out of the phone booth and went back home. It was only eleven o'clock then. By now it's twelve, and I'm already so jittery I can hardly write. I don't know what I'll be like by two.

13

Well, it's over. Everything's over. No, actually nothing's really *over*. But it all feels different since I went to meet Blanche.

She wasn't wearing her red jacket, but once I saw her sitting there on the bench outside the fourth floor offices I remembered her eyebrows, and her square, solid shape. And her expression—a sort of set-jawed I-dare-you-to-make-me-smile look.

"You're Marianne?" she demanded. I admitted it and sat down, and she looked me over grimly. "Marianne—Jackson, wasn't it? From Northeast Stark. Yes. How old are you, Marianne?"

"Tw— well, nearly thirteen."

She nodded as if I had confirmed her worst fears, and took charge of the conversation. "All right. We're here to talk about my nephew, Robert Shelby. To begin with you can tell me where he is."

I took a long breath and said, "Miss—I mean, Ms.—Mitchell, that's just what I *can't* do. Yet."

"What do you mean, *yet?*"

"Until I know how you feel about—what's happened."

"How I *feel* about it?" She stared at me. "You *did* say you

140

know the whole story?"

"Yes, I—"

"Well, how do you think I feel? Out of the blue I get this phone call from the FBI saying my baby nephew—eighteen months old!—has vanished from the face of the earth and what do I know about it? And do you think they believed me when I said 'nothing'? For weeks I had them phoning at all hours, crawling all over my apartment, going through my things, questioning me about my job, my 'confederates,' my—"

"They suspected *you*?" I gasped. "But—"

"Yes, 'but'! *But* where was Sharonlee, hadn't she vanished, too, at just the same time? Don't think I didn't point *that* out. But they couldn't find *her* to pester. It was easier to figure the two of us were in cahoots. 'She's just a teenager,' they said. 'She couldn't have worked it all alone.' Not much! It's my opinion teenagers can work any scam they have a mind to work." She paused and shot me a *look*. "And they do it every day. But try telling that to a cop when he's made his mind up."

I was beginning to understand why Blanche had a chip on her shoulder about Kelsey—and I wished I hadn't said "thirteen."

"Months of worry, I've had," she added, sort of glum and brooding, almost to herself. "Worry about the baby, about that silly girl, about my sister left on her own—"

I said, "Ms. Mitchell, she's not a silly girl. Honest. Not any-more."

"She is unforgivably silly. To do such a thing without telling a living soul. Without coming to me—when I was right *here*, in the same town."

"Maybe she thought you were in Seattle," I said feebly.

141

"I was transferred. She could've found me through the firm. She didn't try."

"Well, if she'd told anybody what she was going to do they'd have stopped her going! And Robert would still be with his mother. Being neglected, and treated mean, and—"

Blanche put me in my place with an automatic glare, but then she looked away, and just stared across the big, Sunday-afternoon-empty fourth floor a minute, in a way that made me feel sorry for her. It was her own sister we were talking about, after all. "Ruth did notice he was gone," she said bitterly. "A day or two later. When she ran out of booze. She created a big scene, which she's very good at, and got the police in. But she couldn't give them a bit of help. She went back to the bottle."

It sounded so bleak and awful I couldn't think of a thing to say. But there was something I had to know, and the only way to find out was to ask. I said, "Is she—still—?"

"No, the authorities stepped in. A neighbor found her about two weeks ago, passed out on the front walk. She's in a state institution, drying out."

Institution! It was all getting worse and worse. "Do you think she'll stay—dried out?"

"I doubt it," Blanche said flatly. "But there's always the hope. Unless she kills herself first." She turned and gave me a look that bored a hole through me. "Marianne, where is that child? *Tell* me. I have got to get him into some good foster home until proper—"

"He's already got a good home," I said.

She just waited, glaring the hole bigger, while I swallowed and tried to get some spit back into my mouth. The time had come. I said, "They live at my house—both of them.

Sharonlee's married to my daddy."

I don't know what she'd expected, but it wasn't that. She looked at me all over again, with wide, startled eyes, and for once forgot to scowl. "Sharonlee's *married?* To somebody old enough to be your father?"

"Well, that's not so very old," I said defensively. She made it sound like my fault.

She just stared at me a minute, blinking now and then. I could almost see things sort of rearranging themselves in her mind. Before she could pull herself together and reset them in their old concrete, I swallowed and plunged into my big speech, the one I'd been planning and silently rehearsing for the past three hours.

"Ms. Mitchell, we're a nice, good family. *Much* better for P—Robert than any foster people because Sharonlee's right there with him. We live in a perfectly nice house—although it's kind of old and needs painting, only we couldn't afford it this year—on a real *safe* dead-end street." I was looking directly into her eyes so she'd see how truthful I was being and wouldn't interrupt me until I got it all said. I told her Robert had his own little swing in the backyard and his own room, even though it was kind of small, and then I mentioned about the genuine Mexican-tile floor in the kitchen and the almost-new refrigerator, and that Daddy was going to have a new roof put on next year. "And the living room curtains—well, I guess they're sort of worn, they're pretty old, but actually you hardly notice, because—"

"Marianne," Blanche said. She waited until I sort of refocused on her whole face instead of the pupils of her eyes. Then she said, "I don't think Robert would really care about the living room curtains."

"Yes, well," I mumbled. Was she laughing at me? I studied her, feeling sort of suspicious, but I couldn't tell. At least she wasn't scowling. I took another breath and forged ahead into Part Two, looking just past her ear this time so I wouldn't be distracted. "Now about Daddy. He is a very responsible man. He has his own business." I went ahead telling about his business and about how he never had any debts except like house payments and car payments and that he didn't believe in credit cards, which was why we couldn't have a new television—and, well, everything *responsible* I could think of. "Besides, he's a really—he's just really *neat*," I finished helplessly. "I mean, as a person. You can *talk* to him. Nearly always," I added, because I wanted to be *strictly* honest.

I cut my eyes around to see how she was taking it. I could have sworn she had a sort of quirk at the corners of her mouth, as if she was amused. But I'd never seen her smile, so it was hard to be sure. All she said was, "I'm sure your father is beyond reproach." Then she added, "Does he know you're here?"

She would. I said, "Well, not exactly. Well, not at all."

"How does he feel about all this?"

I told her. About him wanting everything out in the open to make it legal. About Kelsey dragging her feet. And about me, caught in the middle.

"I see. So what was your plan? In coming to talk to me?"

I thought it ought to be plain enough by now, but I spelled it out for her: to find out if she was going to make trouble. I didn't say *that*, of course. I said "object."

"Object! To what sounds like a fairy-tale ending?"

I couldn't tell whether that was sarcasm or not. "Well—I never exactly said—"

"No, you didn't. But Sharonlee married—to a mature, responsible man—presents an entirely different picture from the

144

one I've had of a flighty teenager on the run with a kidnapped baby. What I need to do, Marianne, is talk to them."

"Yes. Oh, yes! That would be g-great! That would just be—" I was practically stuttering, everything was suddenly turning out so well.

"Good. Will you arrange it with Mr. Jackson?"

That stopped me dead. "With who?"

"Your *father*. Didn't you tell me your name was Jackson?"

"Oh. Well." I had to swallow again, then once more. "That was when I—didn't dare let on . . . Actually my daddy's name is Charles Webb."

"Charles Webb," Blanche repeated slowly, eyeing me. "Then you are Marianne—"

"Juniper," I said guiltily. Best to be honest about everything now.

"Marianne *Juniper?*" said Blanche.

It was really getting awfully difficult to meet her eye. "Juniper *Webb*," I said.

She leaned against the back of the bench and looked me over again while she absorbed all that. "All right, Juniper Webb," she said finally. "Tell Mr. and Mrs. Charles Webb I'd like very much to talk to them—perhaps at his lawyer's offices."

"Oh. Well—I will, but—to tell you the truth I don't know whether Kelsey'll go near a lawyer. She's so scared of—"

Blanche sat up straight. "Kelsey? Kay Morgan? Is she here? I thought she'd moved to Australia!"

Gulp. I said hurriedly, "Oh, yes, yes, she did! I don't mean her. I—you see—that is—well, Sh-Sharonlee sort of borrowed her name. In Portland she hasn't been Sharonlee Shelby. She's been—uh—Kelsey Morgan Blockman. Webb."

Blanche's eyes had narrowed to shiny black slits, aimed at

me. I took a breath and added, "Actually there's quite a few things I haven't—mentioned yet. I was *going* to, but—"

"Maybe you'd better mention them right now."

I thought I'd better, too—and fast. So I told her all about how Kelsey had rescued Preston—though I made sure to call them Sharonlee and Robert. I explained how carefully she'd thought everything out, how brave she'd been, how well she'd brought it off—the purse, the dyed hair, the labels, and all.

Well, Blanche listened. Deadpan again—I couldn't tell what she was thinking—but at least she was paying attention. Once she said, "*Sharonlee* did that? I wouldn't have thought her capable of thinking that far ahead."

"I told you. She isn't like what you think."

She wasn't really convinced, but I had a feeling her mind was less slammed shut about Kelsey's abilities. She waited till she was sure I'd finished, then said, "Have I heard it all now? All the missing bits?"

"All I know."

Without the slightest change in tone she said, "And now can you tell me one good reason, Marianne—or Juniper or whatever your name is—why I should believe a word you say?"

For a second I just gawked at her, with the floor falling out from under me. After all my rehearsing, all my looking her straight in the eye! "But it's the truth! Everything I've *said* is true! I mean everything I've said *this* time! I—"

"All right, lower your voice, we don't want the store detectives to come running."

I lowered my voice. It was trembling, I was so much in earnest. "This time I can *prove* I'm not just inventing stuff. You can ask Sharonlee yourself. You can ask my daddy!"

"I intend to." Blanche gave me a quarter-inch smile. "In

fact, I do believe you—more or less. And if the situation is anything like you say it is, I'm not going to 'object.' It's Robert's mother who's going to do that."

"Your sister?" I said—stupidly, I'll admit, but I hadn't even counted *her* as a problem. I mean, the way I always saw her in my mind was "out like a light, there in the back bedroom"—like Kelsey had said that time. But now she was in a state institution, drying out. That meant sober. Able to make people believe she was going to stay that way.

"Is it so strange?" Blanche said. "That she might object to giving her son up for adoption?"

"Yes, it *is*," I told her, forgetting to keep my voice down. "She didn't want him when he was there!" *On her hands, in her way* I could hear Kelsey saying. "I can't see why she'd want him back! Except just—out of stubbornness."

"Exactly," said Blanche. "Because he's hers. Her child. And mothers have rights."

"But that's so—"

"Unrealistic," Blanche said, and I realized the harshness in her voice wasn't aimed at me. In fact, she was on my side. "My sister has never been a realist. But she's always been stubborn."

"Couldn't we—all of us—sort of overrule her?" I asked hopefully.

Blanche stared into space a minute—or maybe into the past—then gave a doubtful little shrug. "She'd probably have to sign a paper of some sort, formally giving him up. It would be hard—very hard—to get her to do that."

"I'll bet *you* could get her to," I said.

For a second I thought I'd gone too far—she gave me a sort of put-down glance. But then she got to looking at me, and gradually the corners of her mouth deepened in what I was beginning to recognize as her version of a grin. She turned away, shaking her head and muttering something under her breath that sounded like "living room curtains." Then she said, "Maybe I could, at that. If I thought it right."

Well, I suspected she already thought it right. Before I could say so she added, "First I must talk to your father and Sharonlee. If she won't meet at a lawyer's, maybe she'll come to my apartment."

And maybe she wouldn't. Kelsey's mind was as shut about Blanche as Blanche's had been about her. So I thought fast and had one more idea—a wild one, but by then I was ready to risk anything. I said, "Come home with me! Right now. They'll both be there. You can talk to them all you want."

"Just barge in on them?" Blanche looked tempted. But then she glanced at her watch. "No, I think not. It's three forty-five. By the time we got clear out to Northeast Stark—" She glanced at me suspiciously. "Or don't you live on Northeast Stark?"

"Oh. No. I forgot to—forgot I said that. I live right here in Hillridge. On Madrona Lane. We can walk it in fifteen minutes."

She thought about two seconds and nodded briskly. "I've got my car. We'll drive."

We got up as if the same string had pulled us, and headed for the escalator. Both of us walked fast. I don't know why Blanche was hurrying, but now I'd thought of just barging in I could hardly wait. I guess I mostly just wanted the first bit over with, before I got worrying too much about how it would turn out.

She had a little Ford Fiesta out in the parking lot—red, her favorite color, I guess. By the time we reached it I was already too nervous to keep quiet. "This'll be the best way, really," I babbled. "Because nobody can back out—you'll already be right there. Daddy won't mind. I'm sure he won't. And Kelsey—I mean Sharonlee . . ." I swallowed. "And you'll get to see Preston! I'll take you up and show you his—"

"Preston?" Blanche echoed, stopping in the act of unlocking the car door. "Did you say *Preston?*"

"Well, I mean Robert," I said hurriedly. "I—we've always called him 'Preston.' I guess I forgot to . . ." Yes, I had, I could tell from her face. "Well, we thought it was his name. Kelsey had to . . ."

Blanche wasn't really listening. Her expression had gone from disbelief to a sort of I-give-up-now-I've-heard-every-thing. "It's his father's name," she said, unlocking the door. "*Her* father's, too, of course. How she can be sentimental about that good-for-nothing fly-by-night who never did anything for her—"

"He gave her that three hundred dollars," I said.

"Yes, so he did. The one star in his crown. Let's just hope his little namesake turns out better. Get in the car."

I got in. By now I was too uptight to talk at all, except to tell her which ways to turn. I kept thinking ahead, deciding I'd better knock, not just walk in—then hoping it wouldn't be Kelsey who opened the door. For all I knew, she'd faint dead away at the sight of Blanche. Or scream or something. About a block from our street I said, "Ms. Mitchell—listen—don't scare her, okay?"

"Scare her? What do you think I am, an ogre?"

"Well, you scared *me* that time. On the phone."

"I meant to scare *you.*"

"Yeah, I know."

Something about the way I said it must have amused her, because she glanced over at me with that minigrin. All she said was, "Don't worry, Juniper. Leave it to the grown-ups now." And all of a sudden I felt better. Though she'd hardly ever said a kind word to me, I decided maybe Kelsey's Aunt Blanche was my friend.

Well, it was Daddy who opened the door. And after the first minute, which he spent gaping at me standing there with a woman he'd never set eyes on, while I tried to untangle my tongue, I managed to explain who Blanche was, and he managed to step out of the way and let us in. We were about to tackle the second minute when Kelsey appeared in the hall doorway, carrying Preston.

She didn't drop him, but maybe only because I grabbed him fast. And she didn't have time to faint because Blanche walked right across and took her by the shoulders and started scolding. "You crazy girl, I would've helped you. I wish you had come to me. But you did a good job, and I'm here now, and we're going to make it work. You hear? Everything's going to turn out fine."

Kelsey just sobbed, "Oh, Aunt Blanche!" and fell into her arms.

As for Daddy and me, we looked at each other and finally began to relax.

14

Nearly two months since I opened this Blankbook! It's not blank now. I filled it clear up with the Kelsey Mystery. Only a few pages left. I might as well finish, then start a new book for eighth grade.

Actually I meant to finish long before this, but after that Sunday when I brought Aunt Blanche home we all got so busy with the lawyers, and me baby-sitting while Daddy and Kelsey went downtown to sign papers and things, besides which Pete insisted I keep him filled in on every single legal move everybody made so he'd know how it was done. Then Alison came home and I didn't write stuff because we were *talking* about it so much, then school started, and I don't know, the time just flew.

I sound like Gramma. She's always saying time goes faster the older you get. I *am* older. I'm thirteen now. I've caught up with Alison until next March.

So let's see. What all has happened?

Well, Preston's ours now—Kelsey's and Daddy's and mine—legally and truly. I don't know what Aunt Blanche said or did, but she went to Boise just after Labor Day and when she came back she had her sister Ruth's signature on the dotted line. And the judge we all had to appear before was nothing like the stern old Grinch Kelsey had kept dreading. In fact she was a *woman*. Judge Alice Darling! I mean, not even Kelsey could be scared of somebody named Judge Darling. We weren't even in a courtroom, just in Judge Darling's chambers, which was lots nicer, somehow. I mean, she had pictures of her grandkids on her desk, and everything. She did lecture Kelsey a little about her rescuing methods, and made her turn over all her fake ID and told her never to do that again, and to get true ID right away. But then she said it was a good thing *somebody* had stepped in to right the wrong being done that child, and indeed it was a sibling's duty. Then she picked up Preston and sat him on her lap a while and let him play with her paperweight, which was a cube of clear plastic with a fuzzy dandelion head trapped somehow right inside it.

Afterward she awarded Preston to Kelsey and Daddy, as their adoptive child. And that was that.

Kelsey was just walking on air when we went home— we all felt great (except Preston who'd wanted to take the paperweight along)—and I decided it was a good time to apologize for all my butting in. Kelsey just said, "Oh, Juniper, I'm so *glad* you did!" and I said I couldn't help being glad too, now that it was over, but I'd sworn a deep, solemn swear *never* to meddle in anybody else's business ever again. Then I said I'd try hard to learn to call her Sharonlee, now that she couldn't be Kelsey Morgan Blockman any longer.

She said, "Forget it! I don't want to be Sharonlee Shelby ever again. Nobody said I couldn't just give myself a new first name. I want to be Kelsey Webb."

So that's who she is now, on her new ID and the adoption papers and everywhere. And Preston is going to stay Preston—which makes Aunt Blanche get a certain *look* on her face, but suits everybody else just fine.

I think Daddy's got used to the idea that his wife is still not quite twenty—or else he's just decided to live with it. I don't see what difference it makes, and Kelsey doesn't either. She's the same person he married, whatever her age. And they're going to stay married, I'm sure of that.

I'm *not* so sure he's ever understood why she was afraid to trust him, or that he'll ever feel *exactly* the same about trusting her. He doesn't say anything, but he studies her sometimes, and I can see it come over him again, and he has to get busy at something to shove it away.

She knows she hurt him. We talked about it once. She said, "Juniper, nobody can wipe out what's past. But I'm gonna make certain of the future, you can bet your ten million bucks on that. He'll find out he can trust me, because I'll show him. I'll never tell him another lie—not this year, not next year, not ever again. And even if it takes a long, long time, he'll finally know he can count on it." That's what she said, and I could tell that's exactly what she'll do.

We talk a lot, now, Kelsey and I. I tell her things, and she tells me. She's helping me with math. In fact I took algebra instead of regular math because she said she thought I'd like it. The funny thing is, I do—so far, anyway. I think it's because it's mostly full of letters instead of numbers. Letters are Juniper-friendly. I'm trying to get better with numbers, too. Alison says why torture yourself unless you have to, but Kelsey says it's time I got busy and learned some math skills, because I'll need them in high school. Pete decided she had a good point and signed up for algebra, too.

The new baby's due in March, maybe right on Alison's

birthday. She's hoping so, anyway. She and Pete and I are in most of the same classes—though he took speech for his elective instead of journalism like us, and of course Alison always takes band. And later this month another author's coming to speak to eighth grade English. This one writes fantasy romances. Alison says they might be easier to write than mysteries, and why don't we try one? I mumbled, "Well, I'll think about it," but the fact is, I've had enough if not too much of inventing fantasies. Anyway, I plan to be too busy with that algebra. And plain real life.

Kelsey and Preston are both looking different nowadays because their dark-dyed hair has nearly all grown out. She cut hers real, real short to get rid of the brown ends, and the new style looks great on her. Daddy loves her as a redhead. Well, he loved her as a brunette, too. But she's more special her natural way. And Preston! With those red-gold curls and big brown eyes—I wish Margo could see him, she'd lose her mind.

I still think about Margo a lot.

Well, I always will. But it's got so it doesn't hurt as much. I mean, I used to think: If Margo could see us—Daddy and me—living here all alone in her house with the red door, she'd feel so lonesome for us, so sorry she'd had to leave. But I don't think that anymore. Now, I think if she could see us—Daddy and me and Kelsey and Preston, all of us here together, she wouldn't be sad at all.

I believe she'd say things were starting to go just fine.